I0630595

THE WOMAN WHO LIVED AMONGST THE CANNIBALS

or

Camille

A novel by Robert Kloss

Art by Matt Kish

To Herman Melville, Virginia Woolf,

Apichatpong Weerasethakul, & Andrei Tarkovsky

.

At this hour, what is dead is restless
and what is living is burning.
—Li-Young Lee,
This Hour and What is Dead

You close your eyes—

Here a cave flickering—shadows—Here faces painted—red, black, green—Here expressions—fevers—bones cluttered—lions—caribou— bones of goats—And here what was—these rags, trousers once—this skull—turned now so the light knows—turned so the shadow forgets— This skull, now the eyes, lighted, now the eyes, torchlight alone—

You forget by your fourth birthday these first memories—shifting—
your father's goats at their graze—black tongues—chickens pranc-
ing and clucking—grasshoppers in trembling grasses—tobacco juice
stains your palms. You forget the night you wake to a goat's anguished
call—screaming the devil had come for your soul. And you never know
the body of that same goat—sprawled—eviscerated—white vacant
eyes—your father crouched before it, cursing. You forget your mother
fallen into fever—the dull lump of flesh—a shape unmoving—And you
forget the place of your mother's repose, the soil freshly mounded—
your father before this place, how he did seem there to sleep—And perhaps asleep he had been for by morning he had risen and departed—
Never does he return—You forget your offerings before the mound,
bluing bread, saucers of milk—flies ambling—And you forget if those
gifts were meant to feed your mother or as an offering to the god whose
boundless soul housed her now. And you forget those days to follow—
gray withered boards of the porch where you sit watching the goatless
yard, while the goats wander the hillsides—screaming—while the
chickens mill—doomed in their freedom.

And you forget the pilgrimage to follow—sleeping in fields and ditches—within boxes, under doorways. Hogs loose and rooting—rats. You forget a dead boy—his face—pale—emaciated—his lips—black blood—noise of the flies. And street urchins—roving violence—grease and filth—soot blackened—You forget your grim filthy visage reflected in a shop window—cavernous eyes—the rotten apple core you ate from the gutter.

And you forget how the man who will come to call himself your benefactor and then your husband, approaches from his carriage—You forget lashing him with your nails—howling as he gathered you into his frock coat—smell of sweat and tobacco as he—There, there my sweet, you are safe now.

He asks—What is your name? and when you do not answer he—I will call you Elizabeth.

And so *Elizabeth* you are—until the hour of his death—

Remember now—your first days within his home—long hallways—carpets, crimson—silence immense—your way lost and then—a room of shelves, leatherbound volumes, your fingers along the spines—golden symbols mysterious—Now through musty hallways shadowed—now a room collapsing with oddities—a yellowed skull, mapped with lines—a man's skeleton suspended by wire and rod—ledgers bound in human skin—jars—infants smaller than infants—suspended in fluid—yellow murk—what strange dream—claustrophobic world—echoing noise—within—

Another room then—bears, lions, dogs striped, alligators—eternal—eyes of glass—bellies sawdust fattened—And when *alligator mississippiensis* seems to shift—you flee to the hallway—dim oil glow—frosted fixtures ornate—and then further shadows. Somewhere—the cold drag of an immense dead tail—

—a flame in the darkness—a maid—The dead, she whispers, are every-

where—

Then—light—Here an emerald expanse—a lawn immaculate—the outer edges—pines and shrubbery—trimmed—Flowers—purple and yellow and blue—Bursting—To the grass you kneel—trace your fingers just above the prick—how did they—Beyond the lawn now a black pond shimmering—This place unnatural—Here in the obsidian pool—your intense curious eyes unto themselves—until your vision does blur and within this oblivion—a beast measureless and eternal—drifting—the dreadful motion through the surface, before—again—the deeper unknown—

Your benefactor in these days—more the implication of a man—On your bed you find white boxes tied with red ribbon—hats, undergarments, dresses, shoes, stockings—garments to wear while sleeping and garments to wear while at play—And so many dollies he does—little dollies of painted porcelain—cotton stuffed—dollies of gears and tin—tottering as if half dead—

His coarse strident voice—echoing—His shadow—

When he is in his office you watch him from around furniture—He is hunched—fountain pen—ink filthy hands frenzied—and then—His hair—white, curly—a mop or an eviscerated poodle—And later he paces his library, muttering, gesticulating—mournful sighs—The demands of scholarship—a toil perpetual—brooding—At night he sits in a light dim, drinking brandy until his face purples—He calls you forth from the shadows—His lips against your brow—sloppily—How do you enjoy your new dolly? he wonders. You whisper that you treasure your dollies. That is good. And what do you think of your new home?—You say it is a wonderful house—Yet when you begin to speak of the forest beyond the yard—Now his lips unto your ear—humid breath—sickly—No, no, never there—You must stay indoors, my sweet Betty.

He never asks of your former life. Never will he know of your mother and father—the chickens in the dust—the goats, their strange wanderings—haunted cries—And so he will never know your dreams, the shadows of rocky cliffs, while goats leap and bay just beyond your vision—flash of tail—hoof tracks—ever you call to them—sobbing and pleading for their return. Often you wake—weeping for reasons to you unknown—perplexed by the thought *I will never know if they died* although, of course, eventually they did—

Now your years—so cloistered—The long hallways—Shadows—Here upon the walls, your benefactor's ancestors, depicted in oil—How you peered into the eyes of this ancient painted woman—that ancient painted man—wondering of their thoughts as they posed—if they wearied in their posture or if they ever truly looked as here remembered. Your fingertips trace their thin severe lips—collars ruffled—Even their names now—their true names—What their parents called them—their friends—lovers in moments intimate—the moments themselves—all that blood—Lost now—Ever gone—

And in what your benefactor calls his "study"—murky tintypes and daguerreotypes—his father and mother, haunting in black—hands clasped upon knees—expressions brooding—And upon his desk, a tintype of the father as a young man, in kaki jacket and helmet, holding open the limp mouth of a lion—loose black lips—tusks—And another depiction shows the father as a shorthaired boy—a white gown—pooling from his torso. And still another—the father aside the mother—She in long brown dress, collar to her chin—a bouquet of wild flowers—He in suit and tie, hair black and curled—whiskers—Together their faces—young—severe—ancient—

Whenever the moment allows you flee to the forest—stocking-footed and then barefooted—across the lawn—giggling—Behind bushes you hide—earthy husks of trees—The maid's voice—distant—nearing—Elizabeth! Elizabeth! Elizabeth!

And some days the maid finds you quickly, swats you red—aching—tearful—

And some days she loses you to the other world. Now within the tall grasses you fall into the dream—now the shadows—what darkness—now figures creep—hunched—Lighted eyes—pulsing—

And one day—the further depths—drooping vines—muck—dark pools skinned with peat—mist—Here you find a hut—thatched—weathered wood—Still beyond, slate stones—names long faded—moss and mold—These once names your fingers trace—your ear to the pungent earth—A world beneath this one—

Women—silk gowns and gauze veils—Men in suits and top hats—locked in wooden boxes—hoarse unpitied cries—pounding fists—futile—

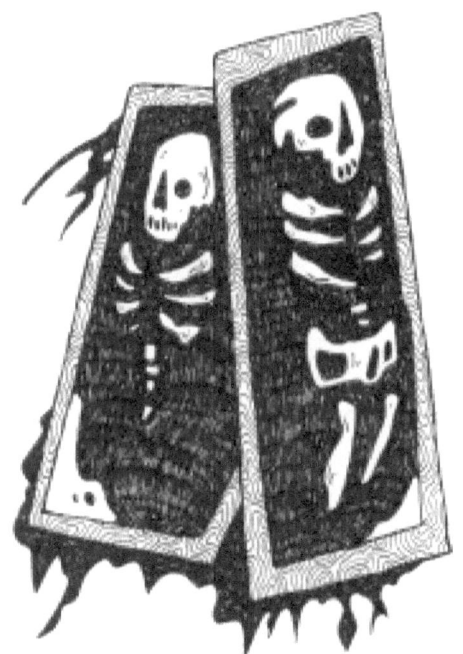

Another time you stray still deeper—shadows—wood smoke coiling— and then a hut of clay and rock—bones of animals—men—Hunched before the entrance, a crone, shawl wrapped—eyeless and withered— Shadows of her fire—her walls—fleshless faces—Now to you she beckons—

Membrane of mud and bone—shadow and light—You hear not the creatures when they come to paw and sniff—pecking of birds—acorns pelting—You see not the wolves venturing—a cautious trot—or the bear that leans against the wall—dim soulless gaze—The lion curled on top—her dreams—what languid violence—

And slowly the crone gestures to the mud walls—firelight and shadow—flickering—She whispers, I remember a world like this.

And she etches into the mud what seem towers and spires and arches. Somewhere there is a city of bones, she continues, and I have seen it.

There the men are like shadows, but they are not—They are the men themselves.

There is a creature that moves from that land into this—in the bending of the light—

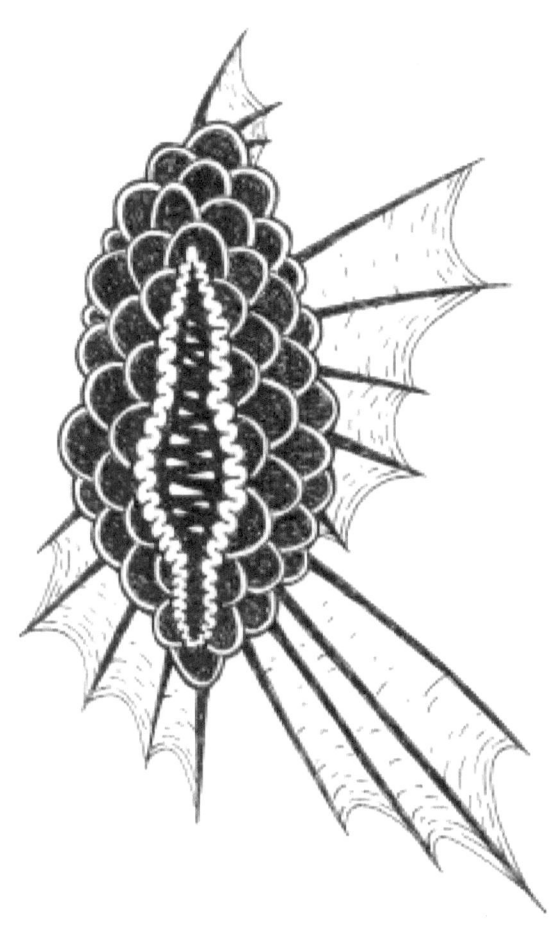

Another hour—you find a squirrel, curled in tender oblivion—She neither breathes nor blinks—But she moves from within—where a thousand little lives—bloom—

I thought if I could bring her to the forest—I thought if I could carry her in my gown—

One afternoon you return from the forest to find in the parlor your benefactor and three society ladies sipping tea—your muddied face—dress—eyes gleaming with life relentless—and so dart your wilding eyes from furious benefactor to shocked lady to shocked lady—Hands pressed to breasts—polite scandalized tones—Your charge is a—she is a lively girl, Professor—

Now your benefactor vows to civilize you. The aged tutor he hires—her wagging throat—depthless eyes—Her tuneless educated drone—ruler seldom restrained—How you suffer. How you *yearn*. And when your flesh would prefer to roam, your eyes rove the open windows—your mind—yellow mosses—black waters—now her ruler cracks your knuckles until you howl. And slowly you submit, and slowly you learn, all the accumulated knowledge of that culture beloved to your benefactor—dead languages and dusty literatures—philosophies—mathematics—the histories of great nations—the biographies of statesmen and saints—Your youthful days buried beneath the labors of memory and recitation—facts and figures—rhetoric perfectly turned—Dead men—conquerers—explorers—saints—What they then called presidents—until you could scarcely recall any other life—

The years—a motion relentless—Now the house once strange in its stillness takes on a hue mundane—Now throughout the city you are known as the charge of a great scholar. You go about in carriages at the direction of society women, one hand laid across the other—Spend your days in shops—clouds of scent—garments of cotton and silk—long white gloves—hats—flowered ornately—

Your qualities now in the mirror you do weigh against other young women—The tooth that does seem to jut—your brow perhaps too high—what of my neck—my lips—They tell me my eyes—

Missives calligraphied and hand delivered—beckoning you to drawing rooms—recitals—this poet's latest verse—that composer's newest—a sonata haunting—Once a clay rough and unmolded now you are unveiled to society—voluminous hoops and silk gowns—Slick young men—witty banter without relent—Immaculate crones—clucking—And in your mute solitude they take you for a shy girl—fondling and twirling you all the more—While your benefactor watches—your great billowing skirts—pale exposed bosom—O how he does—flush—

Each night—the maid deconstructs your outfit and the outfit beneath your outfit—cleanses your face of adornment, and—you hear yet— braying lull of voices—violins—young men yammering—Bleating—

If they thought I could not speak would they cease their prattling—No, no, it would be worse, always worse—

Other evenings—ensconced in his library—Your benefactor pores over musty volumes—old fashioned cocktails—And you your needle-work—your Austen—While to you each the maid attends—And some nights the professor reads from what he calls his treatise on the aboriginal peoples of this land—Their philosophies—ceremonies—arts—He expounds upon the shape of their craniums—how distinct from a white man's—How limited their brains—its impulses—Hides gloomy—hair—And he speaks of forebears mysterious—beings superior—their temples recovered in distant western lands—excavated from—And his obsession—his dream—the obsidian wall bordering the further west, the impossible genius of a people who could erect—

How you listen—nod—What seems your fascinated smile—

Many nights you lie awake, listening to the ancient house.

And many nights you find yourself sprawled upon the blue lawn—crouched before the pond—a mist dispersing over the obsidian surface—awful caress—

The forest winks and glows—a voice—

Many nights a creature does crawl across the ceiling—scales and horns—feathers—So the beast stills to look upon you before continuing—What strange walk—

Other nights the maid stands at the foot of your bed, wearing the darkness alone. And in her cupped palms glows a tiny flame.

How you languish through the days to get to these nights.

These days—How do you bear—pale refined suitors—O lavish favor—daisies bundled—bracelets glimmering—a necklace—locket clasping his likeness: pencil thin mustache—buttonhole blooming—a posey. They compose sonnets for you, the most delicate of newly budded roses—They crouch beneath your bedroom window—moonlit—They wrench their shirts in lovefever—

Before these men—your polite malaise—The simple conversation they offer and the confusion you feign in return—Their faces—sounds from their mouths blurring and waning into nothingness.

And your benefactor little speaks of the suitors save to note when they attend to you no more—He sighs, It is for the best—you would have tired of that puppy—

You will not always be so young, they say. A rose once blossomed does

soon—what loveliness—You will die alone, they say.

All your hours now—candidates—wrangling—offers—And then your benefactor—in the parlor he finds you—perhaps it is the noon hour—perhaps it is the later evening—His face drained of color—In funeral tones he begins to tell you—He has received word—He tells you finally his dream is realized—An expedition—The—Well that is good, you say. I am happy for you. Truly. He falls to his knees now—My love! he cries—His hands engulf yours—Oh! you gasp—

From his brain fevered now—a composition—My sweet child, I have watched over you, cared for you, raised you up, and what a fine, fine woman you have become. And he squeezes your hand—Now I will travel a thousand miles into the shadow of the barely known—I will be gone many years. He whispers, I have dreamed of you—Your neck—Your ivory—Your rose bud cheeks—your bosom—that swell—And when you say nothing he seethes—I yearn for you, darling Betty—Now he flushes crimson—wipes his brow with a handkerchief—finally—I would have you journey with me, Betty—I would have you do so—not as my charge—but as my wife!

Even now—after all these years—little do you understand of the ways of these people—You know to blink and dab your brow—you know to sputter—agitated grace—Oh my, this is quite the—your words unfinished—the air—expectant—Finally he coughs uncomfortably, strains to his feet—And then he—

What does he see in me?

Miss?

What of me does he desire?

Who can say, Miss, what it is a man sees.

I—I do not love him—

You do not love him.

He—he is as a father—

If you marry him, you will never want.

Now when you enter a room—your benefactor abruptly departs—So you watch him from around corners—through windows—listen to his recitations behind doors—Consider him—in ways never before—The smother of his embraces—his lips—the wet heaviness—his mustiness—cigars, liquor fumes—His flesh, pale, hanging—Eyebrows wild— His teeth—How many yet his own—

You must not weep, Miss.

I cannot help it, Nelly.

These are glad days, Miss. You must smile.

There is a woods behind the house. Years now since you last—Beneath your stockings—leaves dead—branches—Your gown—pale yellow—how the skirt skims—And now a light—And now a voice—

Years unto—in the shadows of this house—your days unto years before the portraits of his dead—carpets—hallways—endless—dust and—something ever more ancient and undead—dinners and balls and afternoons at tea—costumes and hats and hair—ornate, garish, towering—

He was married—she was younger perhaps even than you—

Which is she?

There is no portrait of her. No more. Not for many years.

A yawning light—a crack in the forest—a wall before the sun until there

is no sun—what drone—shimmer—O it is terrible—

You accept his proposal in the afternoon as he answers his correspondences. You call him by his given name, and so it is done. He nearly spills his ink—My darling!

The engagement now—a conversation of a scandalized many—You suspect nothing behind their smiles—knowing winks—doffed hats. And as notes of congratulations pile the maid brings a letter—blue ribbon tied—your benefactor's cramped immaculate scrawl. So this missive laments that there is "simply no time" for a grand ceremony— no elaborate festival—white ponies—drooping streamers—no tiered ornamented cake or embroidered gown—splendid unceasing dances— drunken pompous speeches—I hope you are not too devastated, my darling, he concludes.

You marry at the courthouse in the presence of an official alone. And in the carriage afterward you husband's hand falls upon your knee like a lump of meat. I have—I am so pleased, he says. And when you do not respond he whispers, I hope you are as well. And now the long seconds when you seem to consider deeply before answering, Why yes, of course I am.

That night your husband—goose fleshed—crouches in a steel tub—white tile floor—spotless—thrumming with oil light—The slick glistening oval of his head—his breasts—pale flaps—graying tufts of hair. And the maid scours until her hands and forearms cramp—How he sighs as—his back weeps red—the water—speckled with pink blossoms—

And when the task is complete your husband perches atop the commode, observing the maid—her furious cleansing—bleach fumes—He watches as if staring into the beyond, and only his clucking noises indicate either praise or disgust.

Soon you stand before him—outfitted in a gown of his choosing—gossamer—lemon hued—rubbing your arms for the chill. Now—the long suspected dome of his head—Now he whispers the name he has given you—Elizabeth, he says—Betty, he whispers—Now he calls you Little Wilding—And then he gathers you into—his terrible warmth.

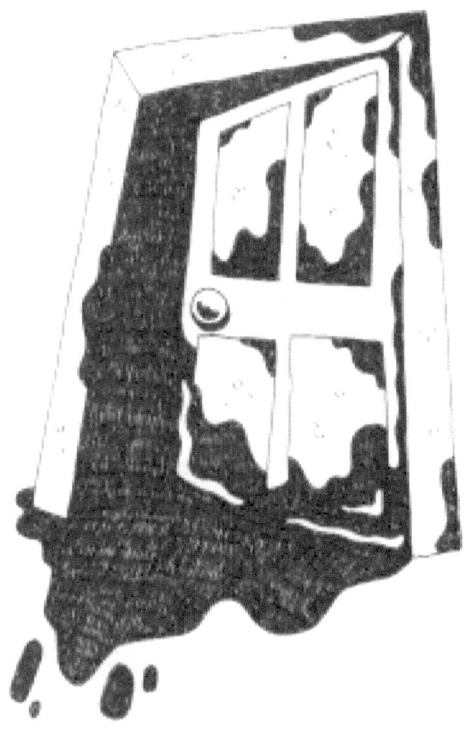

A photographer's studio—white lace garment of your husband's selection—Seated before a photographer—the mechanism itself—Your husband's direction—absolute—all aspects of your pose, the tilt of your chin—your shoulders—posture rigid—while the photographer—Rest easy, Madam. There is no harm in the process—From beneath the hood the photographer calls for stillness—Now the long moment—immobility and silence—and you know many sounds—for no silence is absolute—the pulse of your heart—the motion of your breath—Your nerves—hum and spark—Somewhere a child shouting the news of the day—a flash of light—acrid pungent smoke—

Your husband carries one copy of this photo with him until his death—the other he hangs amidst the simulacra of his many dead—Years pass before you again look upon that image—peer with horror—this pale dreamless shade—her expressionless eyes—shadows of gray and black—chemical and copper and tin—your once face—your never again face—The inscription bears your husband's name alone.

Many items your husband orders crated for the journey—studies—treatises—blank ledgers—quills—ink—ruled instruments, gauges, looking glasses—rifles—muskets—ammunition—craniums—This process he oversees—striding amidst the workers—lecturing and directing—How fragile his precious jars—labeled according to organ—affliction—hearts, tumors, brains—murk suspended—Nameless these—Aborigines—long dead—murdered in their villages—hanged from trees—Dissected—stuffed—sold—The bounty of a new nation—

And you he instructs to bring only the essential—Across your bed and floor—dresses—blouses—skirts—sprawled—And gloves, hats, parasols of various ornamentation—Lacey underthings and devices used to structure the female figure—

O to burn it all—

The evening your husband falls to toasting—his red enflamed face— his old fashioned cocktails—He toasts you—darling Betty—the maid—his generations—depicted everywhere around—He toasts the house—ancient—stately—He nearly weeps while toasting the western lands—the wall—its mysterious nature—Abruptly he staggers from the room, before returning finally carrying a long funnel of lacquered wood—Before this device he crouches, blowing into the muzzle until his cheeks purple—a long throbbing drone articulated—What noise of locusts—He gasps for breath—Now to the maid—Do you know that tune, Nelly?—I'm not sure I do, Sir—He smiles. You should—it's a great favorite of your people.

She walks across the lawn, moonlit—her vague sluggish motion—a wind—You follow her—a deeper night—In the brush you find the body of a fox—eviscerated—pink tongue—flies—And then the creature seems to move.

In the morning the maid is gone—Your husband commands her bed-clothes and remaining possessions burned—until he realizes no one remains to be commanded—In his library later, his eyes glazed—he—It is a hard thing to have Nelly betray us at this time—I have dreamed—someday we will rely on creatures lit by the fire of our kindling—sketches of a mechanism shaped as a man—a person of steel and wire and rubber and glass—a world where such men walk by the thousand—mankind liberated from common toil—bestial labor—No more will we depend upon the capricious loyalty of savages—

The male aborigine your husband acquires—long and lank—his worn valise—He was born in the western interior and raised in the presence of the civilized—In his manner and speech—there remains little barbarism. His suit—a costume once splendid—gifted to him by his former employer and guardian—a man now some years dead—The fabric once black—faded to gray—fraying—nights he spends by lamp—needle and thread—

I want to assure you, my dear, there is nothing to be concerned about with this new . . . this . . . man—Why, as you see, Joe is perfectly domesticated.

Soon your days in stifling compartments—jostling constant—O wailing mechanism—What terror is a locomotive—Hissing steam—The days into a week—stagnant—ever the same faces and attires—the dining cabin—your husband and men of his acquaintance—talk of matters professional and philosophical—the nature of government and attitudes toward the aborigines—Your fixed pleasant expression—the aborigines who serve you—faces of sepulchral remove. After dinner your husband and these men—cigars—cocktails—Evenings now you and the wives—polite chatter—

At night he climbs atop you—at night he—A son, he breathes into your

ear—I once had a son—

And one evening your husband flushes purple with tobacco—Cognac—
tells the others how he found you—gnawing bones—growling—My bull
terrier, he calls you—From this he made a beautiful civilized woman.
He built you from the soles up—Calls you his little wilding—You merely
look at him—

And one night the locomotive roars—a groaning—a sudden grinding halt—Shattering glasses—Porters thump off tables—the floor—the laps of ladies—scream and claw. Women screaming—Men bellowing—startled—indignant—Covered in lamb chops, gravy, vermouth—And then—stillness—And then—silence—Hillsides and forests—vast immeasurable night—

A woman screams for what she calls men gathered on the ridge overlooking the train. Another—a third—Now the men call for rifles while the conductor—Ladies and gentlemen, please, it is just a fallen tree—They shout him down—Weakling—Coward—The aborigine is cunning—dreadful—He will wear your flesh for a gown—Soon the engineer joins the commotion, proclaiming his youth spent in the military—Many years he subdued—the deeper West—His dreams yet—O god—What blood—limbs—fire—

You close your eyes—They are there—shadows—yet a substance solid—yellow eyes aglow—some firmament within—

Men—into the night—The long minutes—No sound—What vacant dread—Perhaps—One woman faints into her baubles and necklaces—Another—helpless weeping—her emerald gown—A third lectures her absent husband—stiff dazed tones—You know how I cannot tolerate these surprises—O Henry—I grow faint!—the others—rapt with terror—a night—no longer star lit—

When the husbands return they little acknowledge—only that it has been dealt with. And so the travel resumes.

Scenery monotonous—abandoned towns of construction recent—
loose settlements of tin huts and shacks—And then the machinations
of man—absent entirely—mule deer springing—wild dead grasses—
geese—black pools fractured—What shimmering flight—and then
mountains distant—snow—Places nameless but for coordinates upon
a treaty—vague cartoonish depictions on maps—The western interior—smoke spiraling from forests ancient—the impenetrable darkness of nights—and days—swelter unremitting—

After a week—two—a black line on the horizon—like soot smeared—

Another day—or perhaps—The servants' quarters—Here upon his bunk Joe reads a volume—leatherbound—His shirt collar loosened—His throat—a smooth darkness—He turns the pages—with slow care—before finally he closes it. When you enter—You should not be here—he says without looking up. What are you reading, Joe?—He answers—*De rerum natura*—In that language you wonder—And how do you find it?—and in that same language—Your husband was foolish to bring you—You say you suppose it is none of his—No—he nods—I suppose it is not.

At the final station—your husband—outfitted in custom stitched buckskins—raccoon fur hat—Hands on hips—And the station agent leads him to his ordered supplies—casks of water—rice—cornmeal—beans—crates labeled FINE MEATS—a trio of gaunt mules—the fourth and fifth your husband ordered having perished—Your husband—Yes, yes, this is all very good—Outside the station—men uncouth—beaver fur coats—bear—wild dogs in dream at their feet—The men watch you—Eyes lascivious—What weight oppressive—Been a while since I seen one a them—they smile—mouths tobacco fat—dripping—

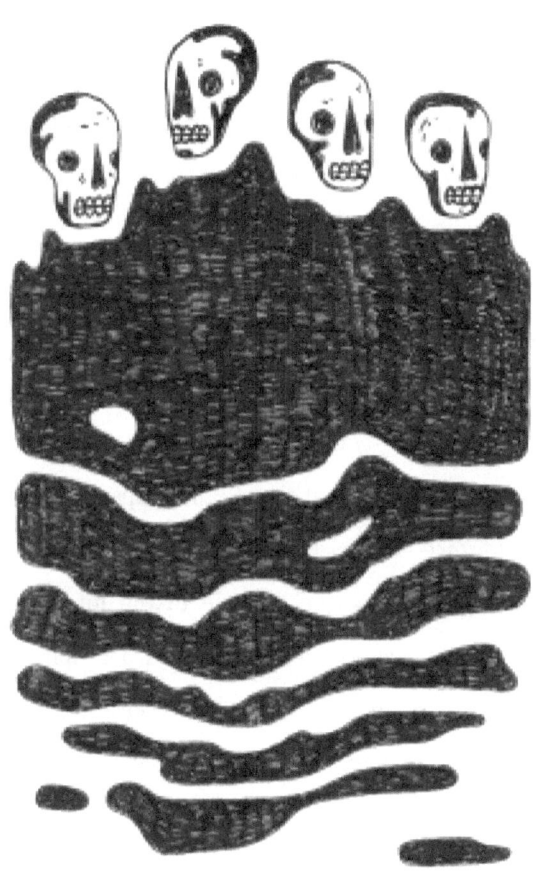

Your belongings lashed to the mules—Into the forest—you three on foot—Your husband—gallant, chest puffed—voice booming—flushed enthusiasm—He stops to regard sweet nervous *tamias striatus* nibbling—or stoop to the mud—a paw print from *ursus arctos*—hoof—*odocoileus virginianus borealis*—Joe leads you down paths that seem accidental and paths that seem notpaths—wilderness encroaching—tangled in moss and vines—towering—Your husband—huffing—wheezing—calls up to you—I'm sure this is only momentary, my love—Joe will bring us out of this roughage—

Your husband twice loses his footing in the brush—crying out until Joe lifts him upright. Now a vinetangled leg—a boot mudsunk—He leans wheezing against a tree—and Joe—You should not lean so close to that one, Sir—ivy leaves—a red snake—Into the deeper unknown—Joe at the farthest advance—diminished entirely—the dark—and the mules stall—they—call out grotesquely—settle to the forest floor—Here mosquitoes—clouds black—insects—humid drone—Birds unseen—shrieking—The further depths—eyes yellow—Beside the mules your husband collapses—Here we make our camp—When Joe calls the site inadequate—Your husband—yet breathless—I don't know what game—you are playing my fine friend—tomorrow I lead this expedition. Do you understand?—So Joe with steady gaze—His smile—It is your call Sir.

That night—a fire Joe has constructed—How your limbs ache—Blistered feet—What blood—Your husband—His gray face—flickering—It was not to be this way, my darling. I had—I had prepared things—tomorrow will be better, I promise—To Joe cooking tinned pork—No thanks to you my friend. You forget not all of us are so—robust in our nature—

Your husband—a blackened tin raised near the fire—See here the magnificence of Civilization—He lectures on—the marvelous process—the efficient murder—Vast herds hacked apart—boiled down—Daily by the hundreds—Someday the thousands—the thousand thousand—Ephemeral life transformed into a condition nearly eternal—the old worlds fractured—boundaries once sacred—blurred—All in this little tin, my darling—You never suspected, did you?—And to Joe—You probably find this rather problematic, do you not—Silently Joe regards—Your people—Your ancestors, your forefathers—regarded the soul of the animal—as rather significant, did they not?—Yes, Joe, they did—They whispered over the bodies of the hunt—Prayed to them as they ate—Thanked them for the sacrifice—Begged forgiveness—Some of the ceremonies are rather remarkable—the accounts we have—Now turning the tin in hand your husband—What is the condition of the soul of such an animal—Whither the soul of the man who subsists upon such a meal—

Through the night—Joe's sentience—an appearance only, for his snores—while your husband—silent and still—You alone remain awake—Save the universe around you—atrocities without exhaustion—bats—soundless—a million mosquitoes they maraud—wolves howling—an elk fallen—The nearer darkness—a breathing—low and labored—red eyes—creatures hunched and perhaps humanoid—The mules groan and shift, and you—stroke their flanks—until again—a quiet—stark—without feature—

At dawn—paw prints in the mud not even Joe can identify—I saw its eyes, you say—While your husband believes you are merely upset, Joe wonders why you did not wake him—I thought it was a trick of the light—and then—a truth closer—I believed it was all a kind of dream—

Your husband thereafter directs the journey—a stick brandished like a machete—thrashing aside the brush—the stubborn mules—And when he finds a trammeled path he tells Joe—You see old boy—I told you a better route existed—He is exhilarated—this place—He sings a tune he calls—Every distant beast—and flower passed—If a plant is edible he insists the group pause—pluck and savor this fruit—between your lips forced—How succulent—no matter the taste—At noon your husband leans against a tree fallen—He is—flushed—sweating—I have never been so alive—he whispers—and then—a voice grieving—What a tragedy we must sweep all this aside—

The day next—what was once a farmhouse—husks—shambles—Where once fields cultivated—now—trees and brush—wild flowers—long grasses—

Emerging from a distant wood—a halfdozen goats—black and white speckled—in their wake—the farmer himself—when your husband waves to him the man seems prepared to flee into the forest—I believed you came to murder my goats—he will say—but then he saw you—and he knew no malice was possible—His goats milling around you—The farmer himself—teeth brown—missing—beard filthy—his overalls—shit and mud—A lovely girl—he says—Much resembling the former mistress of this land—

He offers shelter for the night—dinner—raspberries—fat—blood splotchy—crab apples—mushrooms—soil black—

—through vines—tangled—through the once door—collapsed—fallen from hinges rusted—Here a mausoleum—furniture—shelves—cobweb laced—dust murky—Here disarray—the musk of rot—goat and—fruits moldy—

The room once belonging to his wife alone escapes this condition—
Here a red velvet sofa—Here a shelf—fine volumes—Here a desk—
mahogany—letters—a journal—Here a rosewood chest engraved
with angels—ivy—Here a little stool—needlework unfinished—Here
an indentation wearied into the sofa—This is where I wait—the
farmer says—And when you wonder—For what?—he regards you—
astonished—Why, to die—

After dinner the farmer brings you to the yard—His goats—I don't even think of them as animals anymore—He turns to you—his hands held out—You see—They are all I have left—When he speaks her name one nuzzles his hand—another licks his face—he strokes her flank—The others call out—their tails—He tells you of his days devoted to these goats—the forests—walking the hillsides—gazing out over the great bountiful valley—For these creatures alone he holds out against impatient death—When one black tongue slathers your palm—you begin to weep without control—

The next morning—into an open terrain—purple flowers—cascades of dust—bleached white cliffs bearing painted depictions—red and black—wild dogs—immense cats stalking—elongated men brandishing spears—creatures mysterious—Your husband calls them aboriginal fairy beasts—recounts myths—creation and ruin—This beast slain—Now the earth—This—gushing blood—semen—What rivers in those years—During this telling Joe lags behind—and your husband calls for him—shadows of—

—crimson evening—your camp beneath painted cliffs—In the later evening smoke coils from the rocky ledges—The early dark—Aborigines—spears—taut muscularity—watch from a cliff overlooking—Your husband reaches for his rifle—They are gone, Joe says—They have been watching us all day—He gestures to the forest—They are everywhere—Would you have me call to them—You could speak to them then—Tell them of their practices—Your husband—Tread lightly, my impertinent friend—Joe merely smiles—

That night your husband wakes shivering—Gasping—When you worry he insists it is nothing—Joe merely watches his master—slacken and yellow—The following day your husband coughs—lips and teeth— crimson smeared—grasses patterned with blood—He weeps to move— collapses—His eyes—murmuring—

—he lies against a rock—consciousness—Weakly he smiles—I know you—his hand against yours—Yes, yes my darling—From the fog—his voice—like a child's—Am I dying—You tremble—Of course not. Please don't say such things—

The morning next the journey resumes—your husband—he insists—walks without support—You see how healthy I am—again he is—Your husband leans upon a branch—And when he cannot hold himself upright—your husband leans on you—bones and skin and—And when you can no longer support him—now he leans against Joe. The day—And when Joe tires of your husband—now your husband is strapped to a blanket—like a carcass—pale—dragged behind the mules—And over rocks—roots—How he moans—cries out—And no matter how you plead your husband insists you must continue—And no matter how he insists—you beg Joe to stop, and no matter your tears, Joe refuses—This is a very dangerous place, he insists. And when you cry out that your husband is dying—Now—His sneer—What would you have me do? What can I do for such a foolish man?

Oh God—We will—Joe—We will die here, won't we?

And when finally the wall—a smote horrible line over the forest. Your camp in its darkness—the shadow of—A structure more immense than any you have known. Your husband—How his face—sallow—wells with tears. His voice—stricken—It is nothing as I imagined.

Later—Joe pauses before a bleached cliff—Presses his hands to the rock—How they seem to steam—Blister—For long minutes he does not cry out and then finally—Now with a violence he removes your husband's things from the mules—casts them unto the dust—Your husband seems to watch—expression anguished—while Joe rifles through cases—satchels—Finally a bottle of ink he pools into palms cupped—Now unto the rocks he smears—men—beasts—impossible visions—dripping—Before the fire that night—His eyes the while—distant—His voice—You think me a strange man now, a savage—This dream—how long since you have felt true fear—Joe casts a branch onto the fire—Your husband—They will come for him soon—quiet now and then—He should not have brought you to this place—

The evening—your husband shivers—a series of fits—eyes bulge and roll—whiteness—mouth bubbling foam—They are coming, Joe whispers—Do you hear them—Shadows—Your face to your husband's burning body—urine—sweat—death venturing—And when Joe begs you to leave—return to the farm—anywhere but here—you smooth your husband's burning brow—hold his shivering body—you sob and sob—Please Joe—I know he wasn't always good to you—But Joe has already gone—

You close your eyes—The shadows—arms like oil—reach into your husband's throat—He begins to thrash—What muffled—His moans—

Your husband at dawn—Against a tree slumped—Unmarked—as if—
His eyes—Wide clouded gaze—mouth slack—Neither will he speak
nor move—Not blink—stir—And yet he is warm—And yet—he does
seem to breathe—Your husband—slumped over a mule—his trunks
left to the jungle—The sun burning through gray haze—and here the
darkness—the rapture of birds—Then—the immensity of silence—
The presence of lives in motion around you—ghostly song—Beneath
all other noises—your own sounds—Here your heartbeat—Here your
breath—your consciousness—rattling—and no reprieve—

Within this forest—aborigine skulls—mounded in apparent commemoration—And within this forest—obelisks—what remains—some god once here apparent—and what dream voice did whisper in return—Within this forest—a thousand, thousand animals—Here an alligator—eyes unblinking—consciousness immortal—Here a bear murders a crippled faun—Always ever—in the forest—the noise of the nameless and unknown—forgotten—born and nurtured and dead—murder—disease—age—From these husks whisper flies—and bloom flowers—a beauty obscene—

When that night you can no more travel—you smudge red berries between your husband's lips—What water from palms cupped—His pale eyes—open—

The land before the wall—void of habitation—pulse and breath—How the mules do groan to enter this shadow—You whisper—stroke their flanks—Across the yard a structure bearing the university's insignia—dilapidated—once white paint—grayed—dust and mold—vines and weeds—while the shingles—scattered—Nowhere here the men expected to greet you—No voice—

Your husband—does he breathe?—If you close his eyes—will they remain—

Through this door unhinged—you call to the men you believed would be here—No sound returns from this structure—dust—urine—shadows—The remains of—

In the first room—a steel box—upon a table—wires—rubber encased—coiling to and from the device—rows of buttons—letters—numbers—Slowly you press these—stiff and cold—under pressure now—clacking—From abandoned room to abandoned room now—as if somewhere—medicines—as if—supplies—food—And in one room—shelves—books, ledgers—maps—and in another—the wall—illustrated—painted and pencil sketched—In another room—tinned food—beets—tomatoes—peaches—pineapple—what is called *pork*—what is called *beef*—

Here this room, which the wall does face—No light within—and no furniture here—all absence save the shadow of the wall—Darkness and some dream within the darkness—what mad glint—And here—Your hand along—as if gouged into the board—a nail used perhaps—HELP—

The wall in the moonlight—shines—a thing alive—What thrum—In this sound a voice does whisper—a sound beneath all sound—a name—years forgotten—

Later you return to—you find your husband's body—to the grasses fallen—eyes vacant—Does his chest—And the sun—a blue light—red—And the sun—a line aglow over the wall—And—somewhere—a wolf cries—

Here there are no face paints—ornamental coifs—No shops—fashionable hats—gowns—necklaces—shoes—There are no concerts—operas—And there are no carriages—jolting—rides along rivers—parks—no gas lamps glowing the city at night—No dances—No young men—cunning—lascivious—There are no fashionable ladies—fashionable chatter—fashionable wits—There is only absence—swelter—mold—Illustrations yellowing—the crooked line of every brick—the smudge of every color—every bird—what flight motionless—Here there are only volumes written or owned by the men of the university—jargon archaic—incomprehensible—annotations in penmarks minuscule—Your husband—men such as your husband—their lives devoted to composing dense unreadable texts—volumes consigned to the dankest corners—unknown by most—forgotten by all others—If you burned them all—

Here—The communication machine's silence—The rough unbidden sounds of your heart—Your husband—His eyes—The rank food he will not ingest—The water he will not drink—And once—what noises rattling—a gasp—and then—He calls you by name—the many names he has called you—although he addresses an empty space—as if you in some room other he could see—And he begins to recite the story of what he calls your wedding night—How you trembled as I lay you down—How sweet you were, you bit your lip, closed your eyes—My sweet little Sarah—

The rags you run over his oncecorpulence—Now—How the skin hangs from bone—If his heart does beat—will you see it through—

You close your eyes and—Your husband is sprawled across the thresh-old—He is attempting to crawl from the cabin—nude entirely—Body ravaged—red sores inflamed—To you now he speaks—Promise me—His eyes now cleared—His voice—Promise me you will not bury me in this place—You open your eyes and—you are unclothed—in the yard—You are within the shadow of the wall—What gray vastness—grasping of smoke—your skin shadowed entirely now so you seem a shadow alone—Now your curves—crevices—You close your eyes—and—

—the wall—blackness—your mind—a throbbing—a—a voice—long unremembered—yet you know it—clearly—How you weep and weep— You embrace a mule for there is no other—I will never leave you—

From the wall—a figure seems to emerge—depths blackest—Her airy gown—lashing—She nears until her features are clear—I don't—Your name she speaks—Her voice—and then she reaches for you—

The performers arrive at midday—vestiges of white face—skull caps—motley—some women costumed in trousers, overcoats, top hats—men in tattered gowns—lips redpainted—whiskery cheeks powdered pink—They bear luggage atop their backs—Others—like beasts tied—haul a wagon—painted with bears dancing—clowns juggling—They sing bawdy songs—drunkards and cuckolds—a farmer who fucked a sheep so blinded was he by drink—the sheep itself—costumed in a woman's garments—Others bash tambourines off time—fiddle—a screech tuneless—How they spin—call out—

Before the wall—Their camp—Here a kind of player king in top hat—pantaloons—strides amongst them as—they raise canvas tents—pound stakes with rocks—loose branches—Here men in motley—prance—prank the others—wag sticks up gowns—until the player king—How his whip does sing—How their cries echo in the wild—How they cringe—regard him from postures pathetic—like wounded dogs—And then they too—You open your eyes—you—

To you they send a delegation—You think—if I block the doors they—
And now they circle the building—rap on windows—Shout—you hear
their whispering—Perhaps—We can smoke them—out—Now you
open the door—in your undergarments alone—streaked with mud—
blood—shit—your husband's vomit—One man—in similar dress—save
his cock flopped free—lengthy whiskers—gray—his chest—The other
man wears a gown—faded—dusty—His lips smeared red—If I may—
We—an uncertain expanse—We have lost many of our number—And
several days now—without nourishment—See Hennesey—how pale—
How slack his flesh—

The man—a smile of teeth no more—We hold many talents—consummate in the venerable arts—Tragedy—Pantomime—Animal training—We will—We will take anything—the other man now—A mule—

His voice—the neck of the mule—A whisper—the tongue—sliced and steamed—He leans forward—the eyes—to a jelly—boiled—the brain—stirred to a pudding—the heart seared to a char—the liver—roasted and sliced—mixed into a gravy—potatoes and carrots—ladled into a pie—the guts—briny—rich with shit—Pickled with honeycomb—Stuffed with rice—spices from regions exotic—Stewed—mint and potatoes—Poached—boiled—smoked—Stirfried—prepared alla Livernese—alla fiorentina—alla Romana—alla Moncalieri—whatever rests in the guts—mere grasses—roasted—served in the belly—steaming—

You open your eyes—Your voice—There is—there is a pantry—

Soon men in facepaint—wigs—walk your halls—The machine—They run their fingers along the rubber tubes—clack the keys—They regard the illustrations—Pull the books from the shelves—seem to read—make noises interested—cast them aside—Your husband—Emaciated—Sunken—Your dad don't look too well does he—

Before the wall—night of revelry—bonfires—casks emptied—What they call wine—What they call whiskey—a woman dressed as a man chasing a man dressed as woman—She prods open his dress—cock of ivory—A dogman battling a bearman tied to a tree—A man in motley chased by bearman and dogman—they drag him down—seem to ravage him—until unmoving he lies—When he has not risen the player king raises the man's arm—Limply it drops—The audience—a wail—The body dragged now into the wilderness—the audience waves handkerchiefs—blows kisses—

From your window you watch the forest for the man's return—he does not emerge—Perhaps he—The hours now—Bonfires smoldered—waning red—While upon his cot—your husband does—a convulsion violent—rasping groan—What rush of terror—

Some evenings—their performances—pantomimes depicting wanton pilfering—fistfights—murders—Men fucking men dressed as women—women dressed as men—sheep—dogs—A man whose act formerly—He would consume an entire living fowl—now he must settle for toads—field mice—a gopher once—Another—a tooth puller—outside shops—public squares—he bid the random public sit in his chair—his assistant, a trained monkey—upon his shoulders—jibbering—Now—He with the rusty bloody pliers—His monkey years dead—Now his days—drinking—weeping—remembering his monkey's antics—Another—His learned alligator—He plays the flute tunelessly while—How this alligator dances in semicircles—its mouth bound by rope—eyes calculating—Later—this alligator—unbound in a tub of stagnant water—paddling and dozing—To you he—You can trust this one my child—He is quite docile this one—Many animals have I trained—When I close my eyes—they are there—clawing—

You close your eyes—Before the wall you lie—curled in underclothes alone—the noise of dawn—the sickly dew—The sun rising and yet ever the darkness—You put your hand before you and—O thou pale shape— lost in—oceans measureless—

You—then a hand at your arm—The player king in top hat—red long underwear—pantaloons—He is looking at the wall but to you he—I have not slept—When I was a younger man I dreamed—it was a terrible—I saw a world—the man I had been—I dreamed this wall and this shanty and these grounds and—I woke—I—No, that is not right—

There was a man—from my window I watched—it was a performance and this man—It seemed he was—He was dragged to the woods—The player king shakes his head—No—I know of no such man—He was never here—

Your eyes—You—This dream now—Here a light—a land bleached—
your hands—encrusted with char—Your clothing flecked with scorch—

—a terrain—blistered—bone and skull—yet yellow flowers do thread—the sockets—This dream—a shadow moving—over you—for here move—behemoths—silent lizards—long extinct—Here in the shadow of the darkness of strange animals—what seems a woman—a man—does venture forth—They together know your name—

You close your eyes—The player king before the wall—the alligator leashless beside him—scuttles—and when a suitable darkness now he stills—Now his hand in motion over the alligator's head as it—dances in time to the player king's palliative croon—A light—and there—motionless—the player king's hand—stroking the alligator's snout—absently—

These performers—He found them in the muck of gutters—gave them the right to dance and sing and—Before no one at all—tell jokes that no one must laugh at—stories—no one may perceive—To them he does say—It is better to be a live man singing to no one than a dead man before an audience—

You open your eyes—Across from you stands your husband—naked as your wedding night—His body nude—pale blue—he reaches for you—his mouth open as if—

From the wall come—Shadows—whispering—as if—flies—flecks of—
Darkness—what *hum*—Through windows—The door—thrown open—
Howling—His eyes—He—

Perhaps not obsidian stone but—Perhaps—In heat it does bend—
vibrate—Perhaps—O what hum of—flecks—

And when you open your eyes—where once your husband did lie—Now alone a cot empty—canvas stained—You say his name—How your voice did—And again—Louder now—and—And under the cot you peer—And into the next room and—over the threshold—And now the dead grasses—Now the wall—Into darkness—absolute—

—Elizabeth—

They find you wandering the shadow of the wall—calling for your hus-band—They find you weeping—They find you—

Where is he—my—What did you—Why, the player king smiles—I have
never even met the man—

You—bound at the wrists—ankles—How the sky moves—How the—
You lie bound in a cart jolting—gray wood—Stink of rot—shit—You
begin to scream—and you cannot—The cart continues—O long minutes—Surely—miles—Have they—

The sun overhead—a black orb—obsidian—There is no—

Finally—the cart halts—rough hands—a rag now fills your mouth—
Dirt—Blood—something other—salt—The man over you—His lips red
painted—His gown—His—cock—He presses his hand to the rag—your
throat—No more, a voice calls—and then it is over—the cart resumes—

In the—evening—what blackened sun—the sky blurred—they build camp in a clearing—the wall yet—the wall never not—And the player king orders you carried over—You will be quiet, he asks—Now the rag is removed—you gasp and gasp—How empty now—your mouth—We killed nobody—your puzzled expression—yet how you do flush—tingling—Your husband—We did not kill him—Why we've never seen the man—Now from the others—gathered—Their—eyes—Their—They murmur—Never met him—Nope—Who?—She's married?

Please—Allow me—Please let me—He smiles—what yellow grin—to the forest—There is no one holding you back—You are not a prisoner—We are all free—Nothing else—

You are unbound—your wrists, ankles—How raw—How—blood wet—

When you do not flee into the forest—The player king—to you—Have you any talents?—You reply—I—there seems nothing until—I can speak four languages—His eyes—what amused glow—Do you have any useful talents?—You—He runs his hand along your arm—How thin—you have become—coarse—You can work—You can survive—You—some world unremembered within—When you are told to pull the stakes from a tent—you groan and yank and—When—you heft this canvas rolled—you strain—How they watch you—Call you Missus—Lady—When—

The player king—flames—with his whip he indicates—what he calls his star—a redness amidst—There she is, he cries—There we will go—

The days—a great journey nowhere—A man dressed as a dog—another, a bear—on four legs they run—tongues flapping—Casks of ale, wine, whisky—opened—emptied—The player king trots, singing, lashing his whip—fondling—groping—the women dressed as men—the men dressed as women—those perhaps both—neither—Casks are opened—sloshing cups—Plays of pantomime are performed—a man whose wages are paid in feces—the fresh shit falling into his hands—a woman who cuckolded her husband with a wolf—a performer outfitted as—His cock jutting—

These days—a light bends and then—the confusions—layers of hair—real—artificial—affectations of voice—paint smeared—What dream—genders mysterious—What—cock of ivory—cock of flesh—Bodies—only—bodies to lick—to fuck—bodies topless—without trousers—What—chewing, clawing, sucking—What—secretions—Bodies absolute—Bodies pale, bronzed, weathered, taut, sagging—Bodies grunting—moaning—Bodies in the brush—the mud—what sloshing—Bodies atop—leaned into—lost within—Bodies becoming—other bodies—The player king roves—leaping—stalking—crawling—His dream to know—to be—all bodies—

You remain with your mules, hitched to their cart—you linger—listening—What terror—what—You hear them—their movements—their—Behind you—the alligator in its tub—a darkness stagnant—silver yellow eyes—a mouth ropeless—its tail—a heavy dead thump—

Her voice—You don't join in—You believe her a female performer—in a man's suit—bowler hat—short cut black hair—Her voice—heavy—dark—yet—You have watched her—You—she tells you her name—Billy—She smiles at the lips—her eyes—at your uncertainty—your hesitation—You don't join in?—When she asks your name you respond—slowly—

The cock of ivory—you have seen her employ in productions profane—

Would you care to use it?—How you flush—No, I—I was only—

She teaches you to juggle—from the forest loam a vertebrae—a jaw-bone—What motion—fluid—What easy arc—blur of—hand—

One day—the bodies of two men—ravaged—They wear uniforms bearing the university's insignia—the performers inspect them like apes picking fleas—mere sacks of bone and decay—One pantomime in white face flaps the jawbone while another wags the arms—Still another moves the legs—Their pillaged carts—what was once a mule lies— amidst the fragments—strewn—rot mostly consumed—The trainer throws to his alligator the—buzzing meat—The player king—Waylaid by rowdies, no doubt—

Your voice—We should—We should bury them—

    The others—how they laugh——

    And the player king finally—Why?—

    You—Wolves could—

    Wolves! What of the worms! Maggots? Yon schoolteach-
ers have no eyes—the birds have—Little matter—They need them no
longer—

    But it is right—

The player king—No, never speak to me of what is right—

Another day—the player king—His ear pressed to the ground—He claims to hear distant bison stampeding—We could capture them— How easily we could train them—

Another night—along a lake—the opposite shore winks with fires—

·

Late the next day—a primitive camp—Here huts of thatch—mud—
ashes scattered—gaunt dogs gnawing—No aborigine meets you—Farther into the camp however—noises of labor—grunting—voices calling out—Mounds of soil—like those belonging to—prairie animals—A
clown peers into one such orifice—calls through hands cupped—Hello
down there!—and then to your group—If we had been here this man
would not have died—although from this pit now a man does emerge—

Slowly—many men—their bodies—earth caked—blackened smear—eyes beneath—searching—Soon these men sit with the player king—smoking—drinking juices fermented—communicating through gesture—drawing in the mud—The women—children—suckling—watch from the forest—Later they bring venison—duck—potatoes—in clay pots—bare hands pulling—ripping what flesh—steaming—

—while the player king speaks to your group about these aborigines—their inexhaustible compulsion to dig—with shovels—rocks—blades—ragged hands—bloody—Some sleep at the bottom of pits—wrapped in dusty skins—they labor through frigid nights—blistering days—What inarticulate frenzy—until they can labor no more—Wives call down from the edges—drop roasted meat—Voices echo up—distorted—senseless—Those of mechanical inclination concoct pulleys—raise tin buckets—clay pots—filled with soil—Some dig into pools of water—mud—Some drown—bloated carcasses hauled up—or they revive like startled fish—Some are—

Why they dig—Perhaps they do not know—But I do—I had a dream, which was not all a dream—I heard them—chattering—crying out—I heard them pacing—kicking their feet against the floor—I heard them chipping away at the walls with bloody hands—I heard them—pounding at the doors—I heard them in their deathless days—locked in secret cells—beneath the earth—I heard them all—Your fathers and mothers—brothers and sisters—tender little boys—sweet young daughters—And the generations before these generations—dead and deathless alike—In my dream—I journeyed grim and fleshless lands—In my sleep I wandered—below—In—I opened my eyes—in a darkness—illuminated by a light that—You see it was somehow not a light—Into a corridor I went—

—deeper—corridors—I—smooth polished skulls—spinal—the long coil—anonymous—Ever beyond—a light—and now in the warping—these skulls—the skulls of bears—dogs—bison—and then they were—human—

Further—Deeper—Here—many rooms—seated on stone benches—bodies of men—women—bound at the wrists—ankles—Their shadows flare although—no fires cast light—And in one room—a man and a woman—shoulder to shoulder—in the shadow cast—her head fallen onto his shoulder—His head against hers—In a different room—a child seated upon the floor—I—I reached for him and—Another man curled on a bench—a woman against the wall—

These rooms echoed with silence—laughter—They vibrated—To me
they did not speak—To them I was as a shadow—

You alone linger outside of the camp—Billy finds you—flickering—Her voice—Her—You're trembling, she says—There is no danger—Her hand on your elbow—your wrist—coarse—Hot—

In the firelight—the performers seem to still—and then their voices—continuing—too cease—The player king—His smile—He alone—whispers your name—Now his hand—

What awful tide—shapes of men—women—What eyes—yellow aglow—
Into your camp asleep—choking and smothering—seeping—coiling—
into nostrils—mouths—through the forest—flood of shadows—from
the earth—as if—bursts of darkness—How it—dread fingers—And
then—O limbs torn apart—O—What screams—

Open your eyes she says—And so you do—

The days—amongst the aborigines—May they never cease—gathering berries—red bleeding—what tartness sweet—dozing in the grasses— humming melodies—sacred—no—The skies—cloudless—The sun absolute yet—under the shade of trees—I am cool with breeze—May I forget—death—beneath the surface of things—

—a falcon captures a rabbit—shrill voiceless scream—a gray dog trots across the field—tail flung—low—

These days—debaucheries casual—The tooth puller—a line of chil- dren—coiling—curious open mouths—loose easy teeth—maidens— old men—crones—gummy toothlessness—The trainer—How his alli- gator dances and scuttles—How the women faint—the men laugh their faces red—knives ready—A grandfather drunk on pantomime whisky dangles a child over—silver yellow eyes—What laughter—

Your first drink of ale—your first taste of wine—your first swallow of—
How it burns—Through the camp you stagger—juggling bones—The
slurred trained way you sing—untrained melodies of the road—A hand
now upon your arm—a voice—whispers your name—You allow yourself led to the bushes—What hands—lips—God, God—

And now you watch the stars streak the sky—forests alive—the passage of lights—How you long to go to them—What sound calls you in—How you resist—

In this place—an aborigine who speaks your language—You ask him if he knows an aborigine called Joe—He answers—No aborigine was ever named such a way—You explain this is what your husband named him—and the man—No white man ever named an aborigine—And you say this is what your husband called him—you describe Joe's suit—his suitcase—the books in his case—I know no such man—

And the aborigine who—illustrates—in the sand two humps born from the earth—claws—teeth towering into the sky—fires radiating—its eyes—This creature emerges from the dream—It carries off their dead—You hesitate—Perhaps bears—This aborigine smiles—No—How foolish you are—

Finally the player king—decrees—The aborigines little notice your slow departure—for into their pits—ever deepening—That night—all the nights to follow—They speak of your peculiar tribe—now as a legend of another time—a reality without fade—beginning—end—

That day—or—a body of water—gray—placid—to the horizon—See there those eyeless waters—the player king—sayeth—He orders rafts constructed for the alligator—mules—Now carts dissembled—boards tied with rope—And a larger vessel—from trees struck down—lashed together—For the mast—a tree in full leaf—now the rudder—a broken branch—

Upon their raft—slid onto the water—the mules groan—stomp—eyes—tendons—Perhaps your voice—They'll die of panic—Yet the trainer—Mules are excellent swimmers—The player king then—Leash yon alligator to her raft—and the trainer insists—She is devoted to me—So when they slide her raft onto the water, the alligator flaps her tail—into the sea now—disappeared—The trainer calls and calls her name—One says they see her tail swishing—Another—the rippling of her spines—In truth none ever see the alligator again—

The larger boat—loaded with casks—performers—warm against each other—crouched on casks—The player king—whip—leans at the fore—Now—what merriment—drunken—red faces—blood—songs incoherent—Some to their trousers strip—dresses and wigs—tossed aside—Now they bathe in the waters—follow the boat like—trained fish—ruddy arms—pale legs—

Slow drift by moonlight—dozing—slouched pantomimes—a guitar strummed—a mandolin—Pants opened—cocks—over the bow pissing—the moonlit arc—

His star now—a red throb—There she is—Hurry you dogs—she will not

wait for us—

Later a fog rises—milky oblivion—Through the mist—hands—grope—
mouths—throats—The player king calls for a bawdy song so a clown
does sing—while the vessel—toward the sun—Dim shine—through—
gauze—

Now before your vessel a ship—hoary with barnacles, the masts top-
pled—sail ragged—flapping—A clown whispers—A ghost ship—the
player king agrees—Aye, when she went to port—an octopus reached
up and carried her crew away—Perhaps their screams yet echo—Your
voice calls—Perhaps someone is still alive—But he disagrees—All perished—Listen—The nature of the quiet declares it—And after a silence
the player king—Better to live on a raft than perish aboard a great
ship—So the ship does pass—

And your voyage continues after a juggler is knocked overboard. None hear him call out, but in the morning he is gone. The player king cries and cries his name, but—Horizon to horizon a placid gray—somewhere in a distance beyond—a once-man—floating—

The player king leans over the bow—whispering—Ah my merry man what of your hijinks now—Juggle you yet in—depths—performless— Your voice—flesh picked clean—bones—To what purpose persists your mirth—To what end proceeds your joy—till the end of time—your jaw-bone flapping in the mud—your phalanges—twirling—O to dance your greatest dance—observed by fish alone—in the darkness—Blind—

—skies blackening—pelting rain—frozen lines—And to the great black vastness—the seething sea—waves buffeting—sloshing—the boat—The player king admits no superiority—He orders his body lashed to the mast—Sloshed with brine—He bellows—Harder you dogs—while you crouch beneath the mast—sopping brow—teeth—rattling bone—

So the wind strips the leaves—and the following day you dwell beneath a mast skeletal and broken—An ill omen—a pantomime mumbles—And then he breaks into laughter, and so too—

The mules perish in this way—from the water a creature rises, a hillside of flesh—teeth and fins—and the face of the fish descends into the mules, and then there are no—Froth and dark waters—concentric lines—diminishing—

And one man says this beast was more serpent than fish—another—the creature's mouth—of burning lamps—another insists smoke coiled from—And the player king says—Aye, Leviathan. We have seen the dread beast—And the player king—Had I a spear I would hunt it dead, but I have only my hands. So we will wait—And to the others he—We have our casks, my friends, so if fierce Leviathan swallows us entire then we will make merry—frolic and sing—We will ring out in the spaces between its teeth, until the end of time.

To the sea you whisper—Do they have enough to eat in there? What does a fish eat other than mules—defenseless—Pond scum. Plants. They will find those rich, I'm sure—And what of—Guts that rollick—Seethe—I hope they find land, for it is tiring to swim—And when they do wash onto shore—will some sailor—a fellow who has made there his camp—will he treat them as his own—offer them kindnesses—scratch behind their ears—whisper fondnesses?—O God—Will they remember me there—

The next morn—the opposite shore—Here a fish's slender ribs—a muskrat's toothy skull protruding—the slick muck. Beyond the shore stands an area thickly wooded—Beyond these woods looms—the wall—somehow more dreadful in this land—The player king seems to—It follows us always—

While camp is made along this shore—now the trainer—stares into the glow of a fire—Dread ghastly Leviathan—a thousand alligators in that thing—What I could teach such a beast—

And the player king—prods the muck with a loose branch—water sloshing his pantaloons—Finally he stills—casts his stick with the extent of his might—His back now he turns to the sea—

In the morning—the player king—One of the performers heard him rise in the early—watched him diminish into the forest mist—Another now—spoke to him in a dream—He had been murdered by aborigines—Gutted and thrown into a swamp—yet there he sat and spoke—Bloodless—Opened at the belly—His genitals—

He was—by the military recruited—Billy whispers—to quiet the aborigines—He—villages burned—men scalped—women bayoneted—infants—scattered—children transported—outfitted in suits—faded—their hair shorn—Taught religion by priests—manners by nuns—How many he—Personally—Butchered—a necklace of ears—dried—And then a lance slid into his shoulder even as he killed an aborigine by pistol—shot even as he—He told me he believed—I'm going to die—Finally—Discharged he returned to civilized life—His employ in shops failed for he trembled to speak—the silence maddened him until he screamed—Often he—raved in public squares—He could sleep only on park benches—beneath trees—He told me—He had once been betrothed—What became of her—I do not know—

That night—or another—Perhaps days since—The player king returns—hatless and shirtless—blistered—gaunt—Before a fire he etches a line in the soil mimicking the length of the wall—There is no end. It continues forever—

He insists—He felt—a great shuffling—so he held his ears to the stones—There he knew—a loathsome weary moan—

His voice—to you he—I dreamed of you—you stood upon a frozen lake—wrapped in fur—In one hand you held a knife—Now he held out his right hand—In the other a skull—His left hand—Yet—in many respects—you were another person entirely.

His face—shadows—My friends, I walked along the wall until I could walk no more, and then I fell to dream—

—a pale light—Through the winds—a voice—in a language unknown—
and yet the sense was clear—it said—Come and see—and it said my
name, my true name—Eventually—a cave—contours ravaged—a rank
gust—sulfur—spoiled flesh—And when the cave narrowed he—and
when the ceiling rose he—and always his name—from a glow—And
then—crouched in the darkness—the beast itself—emerald wings—
leather—talons—Now it did yawn a new light—Friends I saw all the
world—past and passing and yet to come—It is a terrible knowledge—

The next day—into a forest—The casks—fastened with ropes—dragged through roadless brush—

When you—rest—the player king gathers a trio—You are the Moor—he instructs one—blackens that man's face with mud and soot—another— You are the Liar, the Fiend—to this man he gives a dagger—to a slim pretty boy he whispers—You are the guiltless Whore—How the boy blushes and giggles while red berries are crushed—rubbed over his lips—smeared upon his cheeks.

Their wordless drama—a masquerade horrible—The Moor chases in circles the Whore—strikes her down—strangles her in the mud. And then he sets upon the Liar—a dagger slid into the Liar's chest—the dagger into the Moor's own chest—his breast heaving—his soundless scream.

And the next night while—The player king takes two from the crowd—one perhaps a boy—a girl—each—young—lovely—indistinguishable from the other—mud and dust—tangled hair—garments rent—These are the lovers—the player king announces—Mere children, really—

Torn apart by their families, warring tribes—The player king places one lover's hand—see how rigid now—Now the other lover's hand—strokes—And now the children—what frenzy—unto each other—

And the player king—At night he watches her from the darkness, while she at balcony's edge calls his name—On his knees the boy—motion unto himself—while the girl brays what must be his name—desire overwhelming—And as the boy—spills onto the—And the girl—her moan—almost like pain—The player king says—Later they will murder each other—but for now there is only love—

He is never not—Even when he seems to dream—he is watching—Billy whispers, I know he will kill us all—

After several day's journey—a house—fire black—Grasses—common weeds—white and violet flowers struggling through—Vines wrap the remaining walls—veins of mold—Rain warped floors—Birds nestled in—wild dogs adream—Here a quiet perpetual—lulling—And beneath the silence—a million insects—humming—strained violent rhythms—

Into the remaining ravage—a cool wind—cobwebs—rotten moldy wall-paper—peeled—In one room a desk—a depiction framed—a man in overalls and wool jacket—a rifle—a woman—three children—white gowns each—Here the oncerooms of children—Here—dust—bones—fur—teeth—The beds—And while—many rooms did burn—what was once the master bedroom remains—sheltered from the greater elements though—the bed—eviscerated—mice scampering within the walls—

And you search the remains for evidence of life—your finger traces daguerreotypes—gray hazy faces—you read a journal—Tuesday, rainy, fifty degrees. The tomatoes still do not grow—and Friday, sunny, eighty degrees. Witnessed a moose.—

This place—void of life—entire—What great dream—Madness consuming—How pleased is the player king—He commands a stage constructed—They will play here to the ruins—the stars—the greater darkness inbetween—And the player king—You see how beautiful—so he does weep—Rather than toil the clowns mimic birds—fence with branches—from the grasses—low sounds of fucking—And the trainer sets traps in the forest—one day he returns with a bear cub leashed with rope—This cub he nurses on whisky—His days dedicated to instructing it—While the nights—He awaits the mother with torches—sharpened stakes—And one clown returns enflamed with poison ivy—the player king beats him into the mud—See how it cools your hide—And the tooth puller drinks a cask of ale before climbing a tree—singing bawdy songs he once sang to his monkey—before he plummets—his face and hands and legs lashed bloody—While the others scramble to bandage him the player king cries out—Let him perish—He will be happier in hell with his ape—And still another performer—into the woods—his screams heard for hours—Finally the player king allows a party sent in search—The performer is never found—though they will travel places where his voice continues to echo—

From lumber misshapen—rotten—a lopsided stage is erected—Now a production the player king calls—[   ]—He acts the role of Father—for the children he chooses two pantomimes—while the Mother is a performer in corset and wig—For long minutes—perhaps hours—these characters sit at what they call a table—The eating process pantomimed—the act of interested conversation—and then from the table they rise—The children attend now to their studies—The act of reading—recitation—note jotting—pantomimed—Before finally a sleepiness falls over the family—arms outstretched—great yawns—and then—Mother and Father—the children kneel before their beds, hands clasped—mouths mouth the words of god—Then the parents—the slow overtaking of a dream—Now this is what happened—a voice from somewhere intones—while the other performers—crawl onto the stage—soundless snarls—curled lips—You remember—yes—for you were there—a whisper—now—They circle the family—You cover your eyes when they—loose sounds—crazed—ripping—The voice now does scream—MURDER—MURDER—MURDER—MURDER—MURDER—

And when a hand from the darkness does wrap your mouth you cannot scream—what lips to your throat—what—So you close your eyes—a redness flares—And when you open your eyes—No light—a bending—a shimmer of darkness somehow—greater than the night—And when you close your eyes—Now before you—the player king—cloak of black velvet—His muddy flesh—You always were better suited to cucumber sandwiches and afternoon teas—We could never make a performer of you—His lips to your ears—You have not the soul—

If we ever cross paths again—I will not be your king but your sworn

enemy—

—house—skeletal—the diary—Sunday, overcast, sixty-six. Sounds of geese in the evening—Thursday, fog, fifty-five. A shadow in the forest— and relics—photographs of men and women—boys—blurred by ash— scorched at the edges—Arranged—You envision the dead, their sounds like the wind—On the floor you lie—mold and rot—a ceiling eviscer- ated—In this hum you—drowse—

You open your eyes—A gray haze over everything—Evening—Perhaps—And a figure—shadowed—toward you now—it moves—How you gasp—And now her laughter—It's me—don't worry—it's only me—Now you know it is—Billy's smile as she explains—I snuck away while—She lies beside you on the floor—I could not leave you here—Alone—Small and defenseless as you are—Her fingers—I came to keep you warm—Closer now she holds you—How hard her body—while you watch the open darkness—eternal and overwhelming—haunted by a light long dead—And now for the first time since—

When you open your eyes—the morning glow—what chill—And where once the place beside you—Now an emptiness alone—The fire you build before the ruin—And still—O loneliness—O oblivion—As the fire—What embers waning—

Perhaps—aborigines—Perhaps—she lies crippled—her screams lost in the wind—Did she stray into—lands desolate—murdered by a bear—legs protruding from—mass of fur and flesh—blood—bone—

You close your eyes—You are—calling her name in the forest dark—in return—a voice echoing Billy—Billy—Billy—

You open your eyes—a liminal hour—Billy stands in the tall grasses—returned—O setting sun—What golden—She does not fall into your arms but you seem to watch each other from across the yard until—The years do follow—How in the evenings you and she—Your nights together—the ways she teaches you to feel—O you almost weep—Never before as this—Her days with the player king now recalled with nostalgia—You imagine the parts she might have played for him—the bride, the lovesick girl, the faerie, the nymph—No, no she says—I was never that one—No—She the sailor lad—the cutthroat—a—Her hand wrapping yours—All that is done—to the end of my days now—call me a farmer and nothing more—

Now—the forest into farmland—and when a wanderer here ventures—
They might stay on as workers—a day—a week—Till the loam—tend
the oxen and mules—dust and polish and sweep and boil—serve and
compliment—Now the green shoots—husks swollen—melons tangled
in vines—Humble dinners—dark bread—red and black berries—What
butter—cream—And Billy—overalls and straw hat—cigarettes rolled—
skin darkly tanned—her short hair sun stricken blond—and you at her
side—And so each day—and into each year—until no one but faintly
recollects that any other house once stood upon this land—

You close your eyes—And here her absence is true—Here you remain—Here you—O the years, relentless—grasses discolored—blackened—rise through the ruin—weeds—imperious—Bushes berry laden—black, crimson—And then trees will slouch beneath their blossoms—trunks thicken—coarsen—weather—By now you will have perished—your husk—consumed—gone to earth—beast—And still the years—Future irrevocable—all this—washed away by tides of flame—shimmering coals—Crushed beneath bales of snow—Beyond even those times—If what was once called the earth does not incinerate—From the universe snuffed—once again life—always again—until the final—hour—

Your eyes—You—within the forest—a cabin of log and—The roof caved in as if a great weight once pressed into the center—And the door—torn from its hinges—

—grasses wilted and browned—the remains of trees—fallen—Here mounds of bone—moose antlers—bear skulls—here ribs—femurs—species indistinguishable—here too—Human skulls—moss and mold—mud and debris—Here there are no markers—no tracks leading to or away from the mounds—Here there are only bones—What anonymity—silent—

—red eyes flare open in the brush—They will come now—But the final

momentum does never—

You open your eyes—O what night before you—What voices from the forest—a language nearly familiar—What mists—shimmering—Sounds—rising—Furious—rhythmic—MURDER—MURDER—MUR-DER—MURDER—MURDER—MURDER—

Here a wall—a darkness shimmering—hand to the obsidian—How it does burn—blister—How you vibrate as if through your arm—a current—alive—It whispers—Come and see—

You open your eyes—Now a cave—The chattering sounds of night—
the howling—skittering—And you walk beneath skies once blue now
dimmed—a gray perpetual—clouds drifting—black smote—in a cold
wind's embrace—Mornings—grasses frozen—Wild dogs slink across—
brittle fields—

—you arrive at the sea—grayed banks—rocks frosted white—silver fishes flicker beneath—membranes of ice—A fractured skull lodged in mud—within a socket—a minnow suspended—frozen—gills red—a strangled terror—

Now for days—the shore's long line—Eventually you hear your former compatriots—What merriment—coarse—One fallen from their boat—Sober screams—Splashing—Laughter from the others—while they prod him under with oars—From the deeper brush—you watch them drift—

These days they wander without intent—They moor at random—pillage and slaughter and ravage the forests—dripping feasts—The player king in top hat—pantaloons—ranting—stalking—Their performances—now without pretense of story or character or situation—one performer striking another—pissing and shitting upon him—a man tied down—slathered with steaks—blood—The bear made savage by hunger loosed upon him—Many nights—at least one body humping another—dead or alive—intact or mutilated—it matters not—

She is there—yes—Her voice—yes—Her body—yes—Her—yes—

You nearly step on two men—guised as women—No care for the frozen ground—sucking each other—What tender greed—And—the bear tied to a tree—its hide—heavy with frozen blood—mucus—saliva—a bowler hat upon her head—redpainted lips—Her gaze—whisky dulled—emptied of all inclination but—the most terrible—

You steal their boat while they—Kicking through ice thinly frozen—you drift into the gray, paddling with hands—numb—purple—until the performers' commotion quiets—until the light of their fires—seems no more—

And you search the sky for the player king's star, finding only—a hundred million—flickering—Nameless and silent they offer no direction—and there seems little distinction between the stars in the sky and those puddled on the face of the waters—So you lie shivering, wondering if you might perish this night—Who will find your body and who they will believe you were—without property, ragged and unkempt—perhaps by then bloated and malformed, or worse—fleshless and as any other—

And had you a pen you would notate upon your skin the story of your existence—and had you paper you would write it with your blood—but you have only your voice, so you babble first to the stars and then to the vastness inbetween the stars—that nothingness—the universe in majority—

That night you wake, jolted against—a forsaken cathedral adrift—
dark and armored with marine life—a nude woman affixed to the
fore—pink breasts—green hair of weed—You could call up as if—But
no—the silence swallows all save—what creaking—The water does
groan—You close your eyes—Here the captain's quarters—a lamp
yet thinly glows—His table set—plates heaped with foods moldy—
withered—His brandy glass half filled—and the captain's bones yet
dressed in the captain's garments upon the captain's chair—

You open your eyes—Here a pink sky—a torrent of seabirds—How they flock to—a hillside of black flesh emerging from the deep—a fin larger than your vessel rising and descending—beneath you—around you—How your mere vessel rocks to the tide—some hundred feet distant a geyser shoots—frothy and white—and the hump of the beast shows—What awful motion—

O god—just—

To dissolve within such a beast—Blood into blood—flesh into flesh—consciousness into nothingness—No more wondering—No more dreaming your dead revived only to wake—No more hearing save what echoes through the beast—the drone of the sea—the beating of a heart—titanic and—without cease—

But Leviathan notices you not—And then yon fish is gone—

Your eyes—You—Moored now on the rocks of a land—perhaps the edge of the world—Here the sun burns perpetual—of night they know only the moon—a membrane transparent against a stark blue sky—Here seals—like glistening slugs—ivory bears, their jaws fat with redfish— thrashing—Here warriors wear furs—draped—They prod your craft— laughing—And when they find you cowering—they lift you to shore—

You cannot scream—you cannot—your lips blistered—your throat—O how many days now—

They carry you—roads paved with skulls, femurs, vertebrae— crushed—Perhaps man—perhaps—And the entrance to the city—an archway—antlers—leg bones—interlocked—bound with leather rope like—sinew—Men smeared with dust and chalk pass into the city like phantoms—They wave pine branches—burning—needles shower- ing—the flame's passage—a dream—in air lingering—

Here obelisks—tusks—the rib bones of creatures mythic—Vertebrae like boulders—carved to portray creatures partly man and beast—antelope and bear—bison—dog—Homes and meeting places—domes of mud and rock and bone—rise from the earth like lesions—Smoke pungent—flesh roasting—Women in furs—skins—regard you from thatched doorways—an intensity born not of fear but—recognition—their children strain in their arms as if to run—indoors—Sooty dogs watch you from fire pits—paws crossed over bones discarded—while cats curl atop domes—eyes frozen in wide blackness—languid dread—

Here a dome—the largest—skulls painted red and blue—Here a man in skins—furs—His face young and weathered—a mere boy one hundred years old—Hello—his thick accent—Pleased to meet you—He thrusts his open hand toward you—a custom long ago observed and obsessed over in the intervening years—His warm hand—calloused—gentle—He smiles—Please—there is no harm here—We have been waiting for you—

Into the dank gloom—the once citizens of this land—line now the ceiling and walls—These depths illuminated not by torch—yet shadows—And when the young man shifts into darkness—his footfalls—breathing—lost in echoes—until even the moment before you seems—a remembrance alone—Down a slope into darkness absolute—loam and clay—a rich stink—intruders—remnants—lie scattered throughout—fallen onto spikes—their spirits tormented—groan as if a wind—continuous—Upward toward a light flickering—an open room—a dozen men in skins crouched around a fire—faces painted—red—yellow—blue—The man your guide calls Grandfather—stooped—withered—his head helmeted with the head of a wolf—his body wrapped in bear fur—around his neck—a thousand yellowed teeth—bear—wolf—man—rattling—

The old man speaks—what grave slow voice—a language to you unknown—He gestures—expectant—Finally you—I don't know what he—and to the young man you—I cannot understand—

The young man—When my grandmother was a boy, he dreamed of a room of stone. And within this room—a white covering outstretched over—a thinness—And beneath this—a woman—still and breathless— So long motionless—silent—and now she woke gasping as if drowned in the—My grandfather—has long been tormented by—many hours he has dreaded her feet and arms, flailing beneath the sheet—A new room—and there—the shuddering of her heart—the panic of her cries as—How she flailed against—her covering—

The old man—his dire thoughtful manner—while his grandson trans- lates—He was not the first to dream this dream—For when he spoke it—others knew—Perhaps his father first beheld it—or his father's father—It is only certain that—The young man quiets before—I too have had this dream—

His hand passes over your eyes—Now closed—Before you—a volume leather bound—a tintype of a young man in kaki and pith helmet—the mouth of a lion he has murdered—and the photograph taken of you just days after your wedding—You open your eyes—I do not understand— The young man holds the photograph—It is you, is it not—You begin to tell him of the day the photograph was taken before—I don't understand—

And you—Has a man named Joe—The young man shakes his head— These objects have always existed in this land—And when you say this is impossible he insists—Perhaps the very first man found them here, before he built this city—

You attempt to explain how this is impossible—I'm far too young—can't you see? I'm barely twenty—And when the young man does not understand you explain to him how the earth does spin upon its axis—the motion about the sun—the second and the minute—the hour—the day—the month—His dull gaze—None of that matters here—you will see—

We built this house for you, long ago. Perhaps it was my father who labored so—Perhaps it was my father's father—Perhaps it was the very first father—He shows a torch along the wall—a woman seated before a fire, and all around her—Shadows of men—No—animals—living and dead—folding and unfolding—You see—he smiles—it has always been this way—

—the outer edge of the encampment—motions of labor—Women carry woven baskets—brimming with berries—tubers—loose wood—Men hack into fallen trees—construct slender vessels—sheets of bark—timber—Now they glide upon the water without sound—Children carry bowls of berries—scamper after dogs—play games elaborate—None acknowledge you save the young man—his grandfather—When you speak to children—when you pantomime movements comical—they stare past you—The young man—They consider you a phantom—deathless—wandering—much the same as the others—When you ask—What others?—His gesture sweeps the camp entire as if here—in the unseen—and seen—intertwined—phantasms—wonder—

And when a child peers out from around a totem—you feign to notice him—You kick from the dirt five small rocks—juggle them with expressions clownish—toss them behind your back—through legs uplifted—seem to bobble the stones—lose them in the sun—before finally one strikes the dirt—The child has already gone—

The shadows of seabirds—circling—

And when the sun falls behind a cloud—the apparent dimming of the light—although never fully into darkness—When it rains you run to your dwelling—and there the dog—lonesome eyes—This dog you bring a bone—and the dog watches—suspicion—unwavering—Later you find the dog crunching the bone—matted tangled hair—flapping tail—Later the dog does seem to await you—but you can bring yourself to offer no further closeness—

Often the young man finds you asleep—in the open—beneath blankets—slumped against buildings—watching children—clouds—what animals here dare frolic—near the water—He brings you strips of smoked venison—bowls of water—Why do you so often sleep?—You answer—Why should I remain awake—And when he—Perhaps you could adopt some industry?—You answer—I don't know—what could I do?—The young man—finally—What did you do before? In the world of our dream?—I don't know—I did nothing—I had no occupation save the occupations of others—I just wanted to leave, and so I found a way to leave—

Soon—you yearn to no more speak—to no more move—juggle—sing—
And when this desire ebbs finally you yearn to no more yearn—If you
could strangle yourself—weigh your body down with rocks—fall into
the sea—you would, but you cannot—How you wonder—What impulse
now moves me—What will if not my own insists I—Here in this room
you long for the cessation of impulse—to slumber and never wake—And
when loose sediment falls—you pray your body buried—obliterated—
forgotten—And you want to no more remember but in this solitude—of
time unmoving—you have remembrance alone—

When the young man—wood smoke—animal grease—builds you a fire—bids you warm your hands—you do not deny him—He tells you what he has so long meant to tell you—My entire life I imagined you as I looked out over the sea, gave you names, wondered the sound of your voice—You smile—You don't really believe that was me, do you?—Now gravely the young man—Yes, there is no question—And when he asks—Do you hunger?—you—And when he brings smoked fish and seal you eat slowly—watching the man who watches you—And when on another occasion a boy accompanies him, offering you berries brimming his cupped palms, you devour them—seed and skin—grit of dust—what sour sweetness stains—your lips now—

He is my son—the young man says of the boy—large curious eyes—careful erect posture—I showed him how to juggle, you say, and when the young man wonders what you mean you show him with two stones—shadows arcing and spiraling—The boy watches from behind his father—when your game has finished the young man nods—I see.

And you ask if the boy knows your language and the young man says, Some, although when you speak to him the boy looks away. You ask if has he had the dream—Not yet. And perhaps now no one ever will again.

Through this day—unending—fishermen lower canoes to the sea—armed with spears—nets—They disappear into the horizon. Here time is measured by the movement of life within the fishermen's absence—a child fallen and bleeding and calmed—the rustle within a fattened belly—a wolf driven from camp—

Here the women watch from the shore as the men prepare for their voyage—rough humor—coarse joyful laughter—horseplay along the beach—chasing—tackling—swatting each other with branches— Chests expanding and contracting as they row, they diminish toward the horizon—And the women watch with relief when later they reappear first as black dots upon the sea—Then—as they walk ashore— boats atop their shoulders—nets shimmering—fish pink—silver—And the women say silent thanks—Before embrace or affection, the nets are given to the women—the fish packed into wicker baskets—soon these fish are—slit open at the bellies—guts thrown to the dogs—carcasses smoked or roasted over red glowing stones—

Many fishermen return only as spirits—wander dreams—Those generations who knew the dead men speak as if they are still present in their lives—and when those generations fall to dust now their dead become as any other—

The young man watches you watching the men—Later you ask him why he does not join them—It is not my place—And when you ask if he ever longed to go with them, he only replies, We perform our own role—

And then the day seems to end—for a gray gauze pulls across the sun—and it does not leave. Now time is told through the transition of green leaves into crimson—bushes once heavy laden with berries—now impoverished—grasses browned—withering—Time is told by the slow chill that comes across the land—The steam rising from the face of the waters—Time is known in the figures of men and the women dressed in the skins of wolves and bears—their shivering children—huddled around fires—

Lit torches guide the wandering—now one dog's tail catches fire—yelping—a field burns until the men ward it off with blankets—bladders of water—You question the young man about this shift to night—Is this common here?—and he says, Yes, this has always happened—but he seems uncertain.

So his grandfather and the elders of their tribe meet in the shadows of the elder man's dome. And when the young man returns from this counsel he explains, In the light and the darkness we see the world's soul—He says, As a man falls to age, withers and dies, now too must the world.

The blue twilight—perpetual—burning lines of red—orange—Here men seem as shades—They address formations of rock—monuments of bone—believing they speak to other men—Fathers confuse the sound of wolves howling—wind gusting—with their children calling out—The mothers claim always to intuit the truth—

Fire pits glow—hunters wait in silence—needful deer creep to bitter grasses—nibble with rigid necks—up pricked ears—Such are the murderous final days of light—These hunters must hunt—slaughter—before the world falls into slumber and dream—Now through those dying grasses—shadows of bears—deer—wolves—a noiseless shuffling creep—Here in the bleak night a man calls out—a creature bellows—a dozen men swarm—yelping, grunting, pouncing, stabbing—spilling the beast to the soil—The hunters return home greased with blood—hefting a creature cool—soon stripped of fur—Now smoked flesh—teeth and skulls and bones in frosted heaps throughout the village—

There is much prayer—mourning—Thanks unto the murdered is whispered—slivers of flesh yet warm are consumed—dirges sung as they carry the body away—And throughout the village there is weeping even as the skins are cleaned and tanned—as the body is smoked. Even for the wolf—the bear—they weep—And while they feast the young man explains, All that is consumed contains a soul—we must weep for what we have taken. He tells you how the souls of beasts move in the shadows—the shadows of the corridors leading to their homes—the shadows of one's belly—one's own soul—And we must never give rise to offense—They will turn upon us—those that allow us life—

Now performances—continuous—frenzied—in the deepening twilight. A gloom perpetual—fires—shadows—fluid—bodies tufted with fur—ornamented with masks of—eagles—bears—monsters still grander—beasts without name or antecedent—yet you have known them all—Drums—the blunt feet of those in dance—outbursts—chanting—cries from the performers—And you stand on the outskirts while the young man translates—There was a beginning, and it continues through our days—It began under the sea and now it moves about the land—It drifts—casts its shadow—cries out in a voice of thunder—And dancers shimmer—eyes rolled into—heads—They topple—Unmoving but for their chests—rapid pulse—They are dragged from the circle—replaced—In this way all but the children are brought into the dream—

You close your eyes—A behemoth lodged on the shore—flames flicker off its black skin—its minuscule eyes peer forth—an alien world populated by the deranged—men and women—singing—dancing—torches bobbing as they wade into the waters—place hands—ears against the fish—Now the slow terrible pulse of a heart—dying—This creature struggles to return to the seas—flesh opened—bloody strips—its lungs crushed by its own unfathomable weight—As it struggles now warriors line the shore—spears—bones—knives—When you plead for them to save this beast—roll it into the waters—the young man shakes his head—Some force greater than ourselves brought this fish—Now we must learn what it intends—

Now clouds—the last light of the moon—swirling snows choke the world into pitch, absolute—Dream—All save the hunters are held indoors—So locked within—the lonesome solitude—muted droning winds—firelight—You sometimes sing in your lovely trained way— songs popular when you last lived amongst the civilized—songs recollected from your instruction—bawdy tunes you bray in the performers' raucous way—And when you weary of song you juggle two stones, three—easy cadence of the toss—arc of shadow—the almost soundless concussion of stone on skin—what drowsy hypnotic play—And with the sharpest of the rocks you etch into the wall—first scenes of your recent past—performers in their merriment—the fish immense roiling the sea—Now your recent dead—your husband as he was when you were young—your mules as they ever were—Finally your own unremembered dead—you believe you invent them—though the shape of your father amidst his goats—your mother at her wash—your own infant self—seem as vivid and actual as any other here conceived—

So the days—weeks—your eyes—Perhaps now years—The young man finds you wild eyed—tearsmudged—charcoal—ash—He brings you across the city—snowconsumed—to live with his family. Here walls of mud—Depictions—Spirits—Here his child's constant mischief—scampering and cavorting—singing—whistling—drawing—Once the boy sets his dog's tail on fire—another occasion he lets loose a captured mouse in your hair as you sleep—The grandfather's surprising coarseness—this mystic who dreams spirits—fills the room with his flatulence—cackling toothlessly as he farts—Here the old grandmother in her wolf fur shawl—murmuring always of death—how her skull will soon join the other skulls—I can feel it coming, O soon, soon, please, O take me death into the waiting arms of my dead—Here the young man's mother—when a moan comes from the darkness the young man translates her as saying—She says it is my father, wandering. She says perhaps you see him in the shadows. Perhaps his light appears to you even now—

—wolves—bears echo—in the corridors—the young man inspects with his spear readied—Sometimes a wolf waits in the darkness—starving—frostbit—halfblind—the yipping sounds of its death—while other times he finds only shadow—piled bones—The grandfather claims that the wolf's spirit howls—locked within its moment of doom—

At the echoing voice of one particular spirit the younger man asks you to follow him—Finally he stops you—your hand in his own—he brings your fingers along the skulls—smooth—rough—He needs no torch to find his way—finally his hand rests—holding your hand fast to a particular skull—Here she is—he says—Here is my wife—

The child too knows where his mother's skull is lodged—he finds it in the dark—sleepwalking—waking with his hands lodged in his mother's eye sockets—And although she perished during his infancy the child speaks of the mother—tones familiar—He describes her come to him in forms corporeal—transparent—in dream—life—Yes, in your language the boy tells you of his mother's appearance—the sound of her voice—how she watches you while you sleep—

You—Your eyes—What lightless light—All throughout this city hunters journey into a blizzard perpetual—the world locked in ice—They return hefting a fat seal cow—whiskers blood matted—They dress their kill upon the ice—the flesh steams—Whispers prayers as—the soul does flee—They return with one fewer of their own number—Now they speak of a bear—ravenous—the darkness—the ice beneath them—splintered open—the chasm—Perhaps screams heard through the winds—roaring—and perhaps not—

The spirits of ancient hunters howl in the corridors—spirits from civilizations perished—rootless—wandering—a devotion rote—a home never again found—

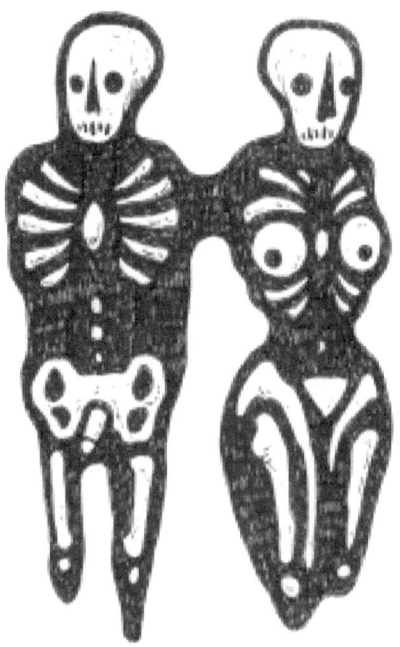

A voice whispers—Close your eyes—Hunters find a behemoth—a carcass beached—more serpent than fish—the lanterns of its mouth—extinguished forever—The hunters have no name for this creature, but they have long fear its coming—A whisper—Your eyes closed—What do you see—Leviathan's throat split—the fin of a fish immense—flopped from yon timeless mouth—a feast too substantial—And a call goes up as the hunters circle the bodies—sheened with ice—frost—torchlight shimmering—

The old man and his grandson—summoned to these beasts—The old man falls backward—screams—the wind—And the young man shouts in his language—Burn them! Burn them both!

The hunters slaughter the behemoths—like ice—stone axes—knives—The spattering deconstruction—Grunting interminable labor—frozen night—boys—old men—hunters—tufted outfits stiffened with sea and blood—mouths and beards—eyebrows crusted—frost—ice—numb bluing faces—Hacked up meat and bones stacked with kindling—set ablaze in tenuous snowless moments—coughing steam—black putrid smoke—The young man drives the hunters to stoke the flames with yet more wood until—meat—bubbling fat—kindled into frail innocuous—ash—

And the old man—bearskin robe—watches the wind rise—sooted snow swirling—black and gray—

What do you see?

The young man's son falls into illness first—fevered sweats—shivering—teeth—What grim rattle—They cover him with furs—his brow burning—yet he calls out for the cold—Now lesions pock his throat—face—chest—limbs—swell his groin—Now delirium—madness—the child calls to his mother—to spirits other—There a man in the shadows—There a lion, crouched and waiting—ivory tusks—

The old man—How he prays over the dying boy—They burn an incense of dried branches—a blue smoke—The old woman follows—her body gives out with the child's—together they are wrapped in hides and dragged into the corridor—the cold wind—their bodies—soon—frozen—

In the spring they will be left in the forest, the younger man—their bones cleaned of flesh—brought to the walls. There is no end, the younger man—My son's spirit wanders even now. He has found his mother—They are together—Yes—

The old man then too—babbling frenzied—furious eyes—enflamed—

lesions—blackened—ooze—

You ask the young man what his grandfather says—He answers not—
You ask again—The young man whispers—He is—His tears—He says
you are unclean and that death follows at your back. He says you have
upset the order of things and we should have killed you when you first
arrived—Silent—and—He says—there is still time to do so, and we may
yet be forgiven—

But this old man perishes soon after—And then too the young man—
even as you hold him in your arms—

And then so do they all—

When the long winter is concluded—a dawn—a low blue and pink—grasses itch forth—fragile—From the hut you creep—dank home—rot and mold—lightless haze—

Before the hut—a symbol pressed into the mud—rock and bone—And perhaps this message—drawn centuries prior—and perhaps the first hours of twilight—or after the fall of snow—

And perhaps this message—a welcome—And perhaps—a warning—And perhaps—a threat—

This language—dumb to the world—meaningless—The authors long since perished—These huts house now only—bones—insects—microbes—When plants grow through the floors—overtake and erode—eradicate—These huts will be no more—What was once life gone into—rot—dust—Soon this land once wild now again as if—any hint of human industry—extinguished—That the human race once here existed—remembered alone in the instinctual recollections of the land—like some ancient vestigial appendage—purposeless—

You—How many—The smoke from the first outpost—a mile before—A man attired in beaver hat and beaver coat—buckskin trousers—a beard outlandish—tangled—His wagon piled with skins harvested—otter, raccoon, beaver—From a bottle this man—His eyes do blur—He does not sense you but his mules prick their ears—

—one dawn—an aborigine clad in buckskin brings you to the outpost nearest—You are fed a venison stew—stone hard biscuits—made edible when sopped in the stew—You scald your mouth—lean gamey meat—carrots—potatoes—sweet peas—here a saltiness—here a bite of pepper—how earthy and fine—what extravagance of taste—you slurp—chomp heaping bite after heaping bite—A dozen frontiersmen gape—a scene too savage even for they—Now you revive the refined, dainty mastication of your former life—And they marvel that one such as you could so long survive in the wild with neither gun nor man— They marvel even more at your story—your husband and your man waylaid by aborigines and you taken hostage—strange impulses—perverse heathen tastes—The aborigine watches silently from the back of the room—

They soon fill a tin tub with steaming water—hand you shyly a filthy slab of what they call soap—Once submerged you sigh and groan—each ache and cut and bite enflamed newly announced—The water murky with blood and dirt—And then your tangled knotted hair is shorn near the scalp—And you are dressed in the style of the men of the outpost—a lovely boy in a young man's buckskin—And these men, unshaven, and mostly toothless—thickchested—uncouth—smelling of smoke and blood—sweat—They make no untoward movement toward you—But look upon you with a kind of mirthful reverence—call you Ma'am and My Lady—insist they perceived immediately your elegance and high manners—They play Gin Rummy into the night—drinking and laughing—smoking—spattering tobacco—while you curl beneath a wool blanket—sleeping as soundless and dreamless as on a four poster bed in the finest hotel—

So follow many posts and forts—Hospitable—world alive—hitched mules—aborigines—trappers—traders—whisky, corn, flour, canned goods—knives, guns, pelts—Carcasses yet unskinned—slack dead mouths—cavernous open bodies—bison, beaver, bear—flies—raw flesh—stink—Occasionally a wife, polite and watchful—a child at play—Before such women you wear an aspect guarded—murmuring almost into yourself—The stories you tell—the devilments—And one aged man and wife bed you down in what was once their daughter's room—their watchful shadows in the night—No matter the kindness shown—ever at dawn—you continue into the wilderness—

Finally—a town thriving—noises of commerce—Here a white house—
trim green grasses—shrubbery sculpted—To see you—your buckskin
outfit—dirtsmeared visage—the lady of the house grasps her bosom—
bonesculpted—gasps—the children scatter—peer from around silk
chairs ornate—All their outfits and furniture—imported from east-
ern shops you once—So now you tell your story—from your tone of
speech—language employed—it is clear that you were a woman of
standing—beset by trials not your doing—

You are bathed in a porcelain tub—Fed—lamb—jelly dolloped—You are
dressed—the old layers—undergarments and structuring devices—a
dress of fabric frilled—ruffled—Perhaps two seasons out of fashion—
This garments wears heavily upon your frame—smothers and sags—
but the lady nods, Yes, that is better. Now one may know what you are.

The eve of your departure—a prominent lady of that town holds a
dinner in what she calls you honor—wine—roast goose—skin crin-
kled—the dessert set ablaze—afterward—the men—cigars—laughter
redfaced—the ladies—their prying remarks as you—your husband's
murder and consumption by aborigines—your subsequent abduc-
tion—ravishment—

The city of your girlhood—you return a kind of sensation. Greeted at the station—cheering crowds—newspapermen—photographers—devices hulking—bursting lights—smoke—Miss just one—Miss hold still—Your blurred ghostly image—the headline The Woman Who Lived Amongst the Cannibals—You are driven home by one of your husband's former colleagues—his horseless carriage of yellow painted steel—cramped into this machine—its kindling—what horrid sound—sputtering—lurching through the streets—black smoke chuffing—past horses—street urchins—the elderly—oblivious—When he lets you out the man—Some contraption isn't it—you nod—pale—shaking—

The house—To see it you know the world that has come and passed—
The interior—unchanged—save for a film of dust—a quiet unnatural—
And the exterior—the lawn—smooth—flowers bloomed—its casual
grandeur—as before your husband's time—indeed before your husband's father—Before the pond now—surface fractured when a fish—
and then again what calm—Your face upon black water—no, no, that
is not—

Days—silence and dust—the old hallways—carpets—silk sofas—the old rooms—Jars of organs—brains—in your husband's office—his ledgers—theories—diagrams—depictions of machines meant to work and think and dream—a man perfected—You wonder if such constructs can replicate the soul of a man—What is a man overall—What of a man is retained—known—locked in essence—the fibers of carpets—furniture—Do the very walls of your husband's study yet reverberate—imperceptible—The sounds of his lectures—footballs—his silent voice—yet in some hallway forgotten—

The portraits hanging—the fadeless glint of eyes long dead—You gaze into the face of a woman who bears your name—Her appearance something of your appearance save—Your expression worn—hair graying—lines radiating—eyes—lips—

This house—the shadows—once alive—menace and motion—Now shadows alone—

The groundskeeper at his mowing machine—the boy shearing the hedges—The two of them—pulling weeds—cleaning the pond of scum—a trespassing faun they shoot—the rifle crack—a rabbit they poison—swinging pendulously from the boy's hands—

The groundskeeper's cabin—thin grizzled man—the boy—sullen—The groundskeeper addresses you as he once addressed you—a child not yet wed—And then he blushes—corrects himself—Madam—coughing—looking about dumbly—he bows as far as his back allows—You clear your throat—This is fine—and then—I can no more look at the land so—The groundskeeper now—startled yet—obsequious purr—Would you have more roses perhaps? Some tree common to the West? Let Madam tell us what she desires and Madam shall have it—No, you misunderstand—you and the boy may remain in this cabin, but I no longer require your talents—

Quickly the lawn—yellow flowers—thorny plants—The careful lawn—a slow murder—natural—Rabbits and deer creep about the yard—nibbling—a black bear little concerned with you or any other. And when—the motions of the night—toads—slow squatting hops—cats slinking—stalking—bathing—stalking again—fireflies—trails glowing—The deeper sounds beyond strains of crickets—chirruping—beneath the echo of a horseless carriage—sputtering—the movement of the wind—trees—whispering—stillness of the water—gulping fish—darting—still further—life unseen—noiseless—a tune deeper than sound—a motion timeless—without wane—

Here you sleep—wool blankets—your hands for a pillow—a skunk sniffs your feet—a cat paws your—And in the loam—beetles—worms—ants—feed and burrow—a copulation mechanical—stiffness of death—consumed—a life further—

Dawn light—Your eyes—Wild birds—what frenzy—Dew—Nelly stoops before you—a walking stick—And when she speaks—few teeth—Come indoors, Miss—you'll catch your death out here—

—something of your old life—Nelly—the cleaning—shopping—She hires a cook—and once you see—a boy carrying groceries to the back-door—Who is that child, Nelly—He is my grandson Miss—I see I—I didn't kn—I see—and then—Would he—I don't know—would the boy like some candy?—No, Miss, I don't think so—

And while Nelly—lowers herself to the floor—rag in hand—you tell her how you appreciate her labors—She—tiredly—Is that all, Miss—And when she brings you dinner you—Please, Nelly, sit with me a while— She shakes her head—I must decline, Miss—and you sigh—gesture to the empty chairs—There is no one else here—You—Please, Nelly, you are the only family I have left—Glumly now the old maid—the opposite end of the great table—And when you ask her how she has been all these years—she does not speak—And finally—Too many nights in the wild Nelly did I listen to my voice alone—Please, say anything—And when she—Will that be all, Miss?—You ask her—Have we no ale, Nelly—When she answers that you have not now you order her to obtain some—When she returns some hours later you—Now we will make merry, Nelly old girl—The old servant sips her glass of ale at your commandment, while you gulp—Now—another glass filled—another—And when you toast to her ceaseless good humor and devotion she—merely smiles—

Once returned to civilization—the latest fashions—heaps of garment—collars stifling—jewels—hats—mammoth—The old occasions—operas—ballets—balls—The young women of your era have become their mothers—Their mothers—clucking crones—powdered and painted like men of the night—The crones of old—into dust transfigured—And the boys who courted you once are—professional men—cigar smoke—fog—whiskers grayed—bellies—paunch—You leave their wives to—When you ask for a cigarette they laugh—And when you ask for a glass of brandy they—One of these men in his younger years—a dandy—lithe and pale—green plaid dressed—rotund and ruddy now—a banker's son become a banker—and when you lean into him, request his drink—he hands it over with a smile knowing—a wink—The drink you down with one easy gulp—then order another—And one for my friend here—

The remainder of the evening—these men—tales of your days amongst the cannibals—the jokes the performers once told you—goatfucking—fools cuckolded—The men laugh to coughing redness while their wives—strict—evil—stare from across the room—And when you speak of Billy's false cock—they lean forward—Did you ever—

I returned for you—I couldn't bear to think of you—alone—

In the morning you command Nelly—your garments newly pur-
chased—your girlhood outfits—burned—Standing in the smoke and
light—your breast does pulse—and what you have been—in those
flames—and what you never were—gone now—finally—New outfits
tailored—trousers and shirts—and with these—belts—suspenders—
boots rugged—flat soled shoes—And your hair again—short—and
when you wear a hat now—a man's bowler hat—and when you wear
jewelry—a man's pocket watch—This you swing—easy practiced
cadences—glinting motion—twirling—

Drawing rooms—now—you are invited to speak—your short hair and trousers—these women of society believe you come in costume—and in the early going you speak dryly of your trials hiking through the forest—foliage—animals—the goat farmer—while the women—their tea—cucumber sandwiches—And then your—an impulse—a wildness inarticulate—A brandy please!—The butler—he—you say—My good man! a brandy!—the ladies gape—How they—titter—and the hostess amused—Bring our guest her brandy, Charles—So you spread your body out as men—Cigarettes from your cigarette case—Your voice—ravishment—bodies entangled—secretions and moans—Your second glass of brandy now—They brought a lot of booze, you say, and when it was gone they manufactured more—We lived to make merry—Drinking—Fucking—These women faint with scandal feigned press loose fleshed hands to bosoms—they cry out—fan themselves—None ask you to stop—

After some weeks—a collegiate lad—His jacket bears the university's insignia—He carries a letter from the university regarding your husband's final affairs—In all your days—girlhood—marriage—you have never seen the university and now—red brick walls—buildings ivy strangled—students in mirthful packs strolling walkways—hustling across the yard—Eventually—your husband's former superior in his office—slouched—haggard—buried under a tidal pool of papers—books—folders—his shelves overburdened with volumes—Many of these volumes authored by this man—His great subject—the western wall—Have you ever been there? you wonder—I'm sorry to say, I have never had the privilege, he admits—I came across men from the university there, you tell him, They had been murdered—Oh? he sits back, his eyebrows raised—What a damn mess the entire affair was—while behind him a freshman places a black disc upon a machine—a tinhorn affixed—a lever is lowered—the machine kindled—a high thin crackling warbles from the horn—The university man calls this the voice of your husband—the sound of his final testament—Finally this thin whine crackles to an end—tenderly now the university man—So you see, he loved you deeply—

Claudius told me once how beautiful you are—I did not believe him then—but I do now—

The university man—the courtship he assumes toward you—He jokes that it would be his privilege to reform such a notorious woman—to domesticate—and strip away—your barbarian habits—your smoking—your hair—your shirts—trousers—your manner of speech—uncouth—what vulgarities—hell, damn, cock, shit, piss, fuck—your taste—your longing—for ale—whisky—your preference for merry entertainments—what were then called vaudevillian—

In the first weeks—his notes—and emissaries—underclassmen bearing candies and flowers—playing violins—singing in tones plaintive—You turn them away—And finally you—agree—When he claims to require some lady upon his arm for the theater—now a ballet—now an opera—a ball—His attire—unchanging from season to season—His tuxedo—top hat—gloves—His conversation—a weighty silence—His manner of dance—He walks you in dignified circles, for he disdains ostentatious movement—

The gifts he brings you—gowns—gloves—For him you seem to scorn phrases unrefined—You seem to give up tobacco—renounce liquor—although one night you drink too much champagne and collapse into him—laughing and sobbing—And another night at the opera you filch from the bar a bottle of whisky—Now while the Moor strangles dead his wife you loudly hum bawdy songs—Weep—When the university man upbraids you during the carriage ride home—Shut up, you say—you open his trousers—unsheathe what matter you find there—gray—docile—And so he—

You open your eyes—What light upon the ceiling—No, I will never seen

him again—

Another evening—dinner at his home—duck confit—garlic—roasted potatoes—Wait staff—aborigines—His daughter—son—his son's wife—children—The son's amused glances turned lascivious now after his third glass of wine—his wife's flush when he—In hungered tones now he speaks to you—The daughter her—high severe collar—black hair without embellishment—Her comments—hatred in her gaze—For she once attended a talk you gave—your rustic attire—your coarseness—I have never been so sickened, she insists—Devoted to her father, she has taken no lovers—borne no courtships—She never will—

An afternoon he calls on you—a surprise—He brings you to an exhibition of aboriginal artifacts and art at the Museum of Natural History—Here promotional banners unfurled—the frenzy of the press—common fools—gaping—Please, you say, can we not—Here bored school children—aborigines—in civilized dress are led from room to room while civilized schoolmasters lecture—The slow shuffling crowds—coughing—murmuring—And the university man—his commentary unceasing—This author of *Notes and Discourses on the Nature of the Aboriginal Peoples of North America*—How he praises the subtle, barbaric genius—poles carved ornately—wooden masks—animals recognized and animals, demons, and devils without antecedent in civilized thought—What sublime, childlike ignorance—their paintings—red and black elongated figures—bison—lions—bears—drawn onto cliffs a thousand years earlier—carved out—crated—Here displayed—And into a room containing a temple reconstructed—stones, cleaned of moss—dirt—sediment—Another room—the exhumed skeletons of aborigines—men—women—erected by wire and rod—another room—spears—shields—arrows—A final room—Here—a fragment of the wall—encased in glass—a pedestal of marble—Magnificent, the university man beams—It isn't real, you whisper—

You open your eyes—Waves of darkness—somewhere his voice—Your eyes—What darkness immeasurable—O god to lie down in the deep— And when you begin to cry—Desolation inconsolable—What—And when he attempts to quiet you now—what lines you draw into his face— His neck—And his eyes—O they say you attempt to claw his eyes out—

You close your eyes—a humming—Burning—

You return another day—alone—the open floors—artifacts—little depth of remembrance—from room to room—until you come to the final room—here an aborigine in black dusty suit—before the fragment of the wall—He is weathered—balding—but you know him well—to his back you—I don't believe it is what they say it is—He looks up—to you he says nothing—

You follow him—through the museum—pausing when he seems to— and then—from the museum altogether—And when he does not hire a carriage—through the jostling crowds—sidewalks winding—Finally an iron gate—a brick building—Here aboriginal children—orphaned by war—abducted by missionaries—housed in dormitories—instructed in the manners—the gods—of your land—

You enter through the open gate—He awaits you in the shadows—His quiet knowing smile of years past—You—I have often wondered if you did live, and if you returned, or if you went with those tribesmen into the wild—His thin smile—I don't know what you're talking about— Now—the name you believe to be his—His laugh—Perhaps to you we are all the same man—You—My husband lived for weeks after you left—His final days were filled with great agony—When you reach for his hand he pulls back—Please, you sigh. I am at the old house—Come see me, if you wish—

No one—Your name now infamous—Your—What scandal and gossip—And the invitations—dinners—balls—now mercifully ended—
Now alone—creaking noises—shadows—And when you thank Nelly
for—your voice spoken and so long unheard seems a noise alien and
strange—

If—none except I hear these sounds I make—will no one remember me—will I—perish as if I never—How I hope so—

And the backyard—your nightclothes—ale bottles empty—broken—

Here the forest growing around you—What creeping things—their

multitude—

—the halls—darkness—will no movement of a soul—wandering—
You—Your eyes—You are slumped against a wall—No ancient dream
now—No alligator arisen to—

—your husband's library—light diversions little valued by his race—
This poet who lamented the limitations of posterity—This woman who
desired the song of women—her lyre—her heart torn with—This—
ceaseless war—bodies piled—flies sing—widows—From windows
they—what nobility—

—your husband's rooms—murky jars—his lectures—drafts of—notations—volumes on natural history—diagrams of machines unbuildable—And you open his cabinets—here more jars—eyes, kidneys, a brain—here skulls, jawbones—notated—script illegible—Another cabinet—Here alone a volume titled *De humani corporis fabrica*—the inscription—The bynding of this booke is all that remains of my deare servant Thomas—Here a tall cabinet of mahogany—locked—Your ears to the wood as if some voice—And when finally you force the lock—what air—musty—How you sneeze—How—In the cabinet before you stands a woman dressed as a maid—suspended in repose eternal—Her skin grayed and hair wiry—her eyes of glass and lips sewn shut—You scream and—and you cannot stop—Nelly stands behind you—to the gray still features now her fingers—gently—I knew—I knew you were here—

I do not remember—her voice—Her weariness—yes—her weariness when she did not know I—stolen moments when her shoulders sagged—Sometimes she sang to me—a language I did not know—I dared not ask what the words meant—I remember her face in the oven light—her ragged hands—I remember how she seemed to not remember Father—how she never said his name while he—but she was always waiting for him—until finally he came from the forest—entered through the backdoor—until finally he returned in his overalls—He smelled of sweat—soil—How filthy he—Then she embraced him—and then she said his name—

Unto a wheelbarrow—jars of organs—the body—bedsheet wrapped—
Through the forest Nelly leads you—Here a building of granite stretched
green with moss and ivy—Housed here the banker turned pilgrim who
subdued a brute world by lash and musket—his first wife cold and distant and then dead of fever—the wife to follow, the young one—dead
soon in childbirth—

Still farther—an area burnished with deadfall and dead leaves—the
wide swatch of land—Now she stops—Here are mine, she says—Her
grandmother—Her grandfather—The exact area of repose uncertain—
So here you dig through the waning hours—And when the soil is heaped
and mounded to your waist you settle the body within—roots and rocks
and dankness pungent—Onto the shroud you place the jars—and
then the soil layered—Finally—a wooden marker inscribed—NELLY'S
MOTHER—

And when—that evening Nelly is gone. And no matter the hours you
await her return—and no matter your search for a note—No, she is
gone—absolute—

O god if only—if only they had smothered me in the cradle—

Eventually the cook—She seems to speak to the floor—her hands clasped—Ma'am, I—Go away, you moan—Ma'am, there is no food in the—I said go away. Unless you have ale—have you ale?—She begins to—and then she says something of how Nelly's grandson once acquired the goods, and now that they are gone—You moan again—Can't you just manage it yourself?—I would but I—I can't work that contraption Ma'am—Your eyes—they—Contraption?—The automobile, ma'am—Now you sit up—We have an automobile?—

Before the device—dressing gown—bare feet—in the stables where your husband once housed the carriage—his horses—The cook stands behind you and—You say, It is monstrous—you run your fingers along the frame—black paint—and then you open the door—the stiff slow swing—and—cramped—uncomfortable—you settle into the driver's seat—How frail this device seems—How uncertain—What madness to hurtle within—How does one . . . start it? you ask. The cook says she knows nothing of it—Did you never watch . . . them?—The cook claims she did not. So there you sit, your hands occasionally resting upon the wheel—It is monstrous, you mumble—your chest rises and falls—you think, We must have it destroyed—You turn to the cook—Hire someone to make this machine move—For the longest while the cook shifts uncertainly, before—Yes, Ma'am—

Her nephew—a lanky boy of about fifteen—silent before you—his faded suit—scuffed black shoes—He shifts in place—as if he longs only to tear from his garment and run into the forest—You recall such energy—writhing and bursting—the immortal soul not yet subdued by the mortal malaise. And you want to say that this boy should not move in machines when youth deserves some profound task—a journey horrifying—but instead you wonder—He can drive this thing?—Now the boy demonstrates—his knees jammed against the wheel—a roaring horrid—sputtering—gusting smoke—the machine careens—It is a beastly contraption, you mutter—He seems to go rather fast—The cook nods—That is the manner of the device, Ma'am—

Only once do you ride in this—The boy—attired in new cap—new suit—
new glinting shoes—he calls you Madam—bows sweepingly when you
near—Yes, how gallant—until the machine is kindled—his driving
goggles affixed—for now you hurtle into the world—a brute roaring
missile of steel—rubber—fumes—limited by nothing—not time nor
space—fear of mortal doom—

Here a woman—her parasol—crossing a street—she must either
leap from the road or perish—a man on a bicycle—this fellow the boy
swerves past—The boy confronts an automobile from the opposite
direction—cackles when the other driver swerves—the final instant—
And here the boy passes all other automobiles—the roar and fumes—
the remorseless bouncing—jolting—shuddering—the concussion of
the wind—insects—what spattering murder—Finally a high barking
noise—you—O god it is falling apart—until you realize the boy is shouting some gay popular tune—What grin of maniacal glee—you begin to
scream—

You house the driver in the groundskeeper's old cabin—Never before away from his family—His one frayed suit—shoes scuffed—his possessions—a single satchel—his posture stiff—expression impassive—In silence you direct him through the tangled yard—the cabin, weathered and dismal—the shingles stripped—a window smashed in. We will—I will see that it is tidied up some, you murmur—It is fine already Ma'am, he says.

The door is opened—Here—a wilding girl—contented dozing face—milk pale calves—Her feet black with dirt—ash—White tattered dress—filth smeared—Curled on the floor—her hands for a pillow—eyelids fluttering—Pink lips—parted slightly—The driver—but you put a hand to his arm—No, no—The girl yet sleeping—then her eyes—wide—black—You stroke her arm—It's all right, lovely—She watches you as if—before whispering—Food—and then in a voice stronger—Please, Missus, I'm starving—How you nod—Yes, I know—all that is over now, my lovely girl—

Soon the wilding—before plates heaped with potatoes—chicken—chocolate cake—She clasps her utensils as if uncertain of their function—Watching you—the corner of her eye—she lifts to her lips dainty hesitant bites—until you say, It is alright—pretend I am not here—Missus?—You nod—Now she with fingers—devours—cake—potatoes—skin—flesh—the bones she gnaws—licks her fingers—black with cake smear—

Your voice—almost a whisper—You have been alone in the wild for some while?

Face stuffed, she nods—

You have no father—

She nods—

You have no mother—

She—

What is your name?

She does not know—she has roamed a great distance—been a ward to many—borne many designations—guises—

I see. Yes. I understand. Then I think I will call you Camille—

You close your eyes—Before you—a porcelain clawfoot tub filled—
steam does rise from the face of the waters—You will feel much better,
you tell her—The wilding seems to nod—You leave her, and outside you
wait—how long the minutes—finally—you knock upon the door—And
when you hear no answer, you open the door—She is still standing—
clothing at her feet—her slim pale buttocks—ribs—shoulder bones—
grim wings—when she turns—belly's paucity—red welts—bites everywhere—Her eyes well with tears—now her arms crossed before her
breast uncross to wipe those tears—She—I—

Now your hand—her elbow—your fingers—the ridge of her ribs—Your
voice—how soft—Toe first my dear—Slowly now—the nails over-
grown—dirt encrusted—into the water—Now an ankle—then the
calf—her knees—her breasts—chin—Her eyes the while—intense—
calculating—wild—perhaps prepared to dart from the room—In your
hand—a sponge coarse—Will you let me wash you?—she inspects the
pores—Slowly she nods—and so you—

And when—you open your eyes—her body in the darkness—Slender shape—nightgown—your own, once—What smell of dust and time—How small her ears—her freckles—How pale—Her quiet voice when she thanks you—your thousand kindnesses—The house a dream—You leave her in your childhood bed—

In the morning you find her—barefooted, tiptoes peeking out from under her nightgown—Lost in the eyes of the dead—she does not know you are—Quietly you say her name—again—Finally then she flinches, turns—She begins to apologize but you—When I was a girl—I saw many things in these halls, and I too was drawn to these portraits—And when Camille—this man in his ruffled collar—gown of armor or that stern immaculate woman—painted face—you explain this one was a duke in the old country—that one ordered this house built—When—the portrait of you and your husband—That was me, a long time ago. I was only a little older than you probably are today—Camille looks at you—the portrait—and you again—Is that your father?—You begin to speak and then—No, no, you finally say. That man was—he was many things, I suppose. This was his home, in fact, and I came into it only after his passing. The rest of these people—they are his family—Camille then— Where is he now?—He died in the west and there he remains, I'm afraid. He's been there many years ago now.

Days then—Your dress her in your outfits—Slim—delicate—shirts and trousers too large hang—confusedly—She fights you not—And when you sheer her hair, rife with infestation, to a length similar to your own—She does not weep—thrash—Gladly she follow you into—tall grasses—wild flowers—a picnic basket in one hand—you hook your arm in hers—when you stop to smell—a crimson flower—She says— How pretty, what is it called?—It doesn't have a name—Let's name it then—You smile—No, let's leave our flower as she is—

Many afternoons—now—You curl with each other in the field—grasses about you—creeping things—gathering—feeding—mating—Sun without relent—birds—shadow swooping—clouds—you—This one an airship—this other—a sea vessel—What sandwiches the cook packed—roast beef thinly sliced—lamb with catsup—and sweet marmalade—cheese—You each—Her lips—tongue—Yours—

Your voice—She—O Godesse, (for such I take thee—thy face terrestri-all—Nor voyce sound—I—Such wounded beast as—But every modern god will—His vast prerogative—To rage, to lust, to commend,—god of love—wakened—To ungod this child again,—I should love her who loves not me—Look in thy glass—tell the face thou—Now—that face should form—Whose fresh repair—Thou dost beguile the world, unbless—She nods—She—She does seem to listen—

—your adventures in the wild—her own—Hours transient—Illusion of days—hands entwined—your voices—What sound—lost now—Your hearts—what pulse—No more—your breath—rhythm—

O—a bawdy song you scarcely remember—juggle four small stones—
how quickly they scatter to the ground—I'm a touch out of practice—
Camille applauds all the same—Whistles—

And Camille—Why did you not remain with them—merry and strange—Why did you return to this awful place—She says—If I ever get away from them—all the priests—dogooders—rules—I'll never come back—I would rather live in a hut—mud—leaves—I would rather eat berries all day—than listen to some old buzzard yap and croak on—about god—or read their awful old books—mop their floors—let some old fool climb atop me—

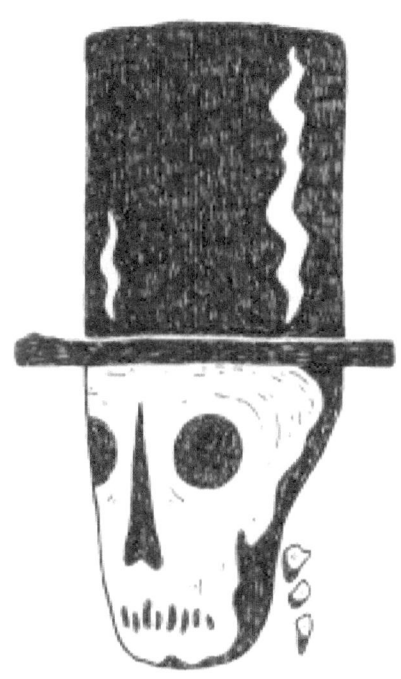

I do not know, my darling. Perhaps the answer is I lack your courage—

One evening—a traveling show—Here a rude theater—dim—smoky—
Here—performing dogs—poodles—blue ribbons trimmed—bounding through hoops—Here a man—smiling—his tuxedo—a wooden
boy seated upon his lap—the boy's clacking mouth—high ghastly
voice—Here a trio of brothers—false beards—mustaches—rude
jokes—pranks ceaseless—this man kicked in the ass—that man swindled—this woman chased by a man honking a horn—How Camille
snorts and groans—slaps her knee—When you ask during the auto
ride home—What did you think, my darling?—she grabs your arm—
her delight—They were amazing!—

Here the moving picture show—when Camille insists you take her—the velvet curtain pulled open—a light mysterious over the audience—the screen—flickering world—The first picture—a bandit running from a locomotive—The locomotive, mammoth—gusting steam—throttles toward the screen—How you barely suppress a scream—the urge to run—Another picture—a gangster chasing a little boy—a piano accompaniment—How the audience laughs when he totters and slips—when the boy strikes him with a frying pan—birds flutter about his head— And then—a car chase ending in a wreck—bodies piled—angels rising in white gowns—Another—a man—a vagrant—his pants ever falling to his ankles—always his dignity—cigar butts from the street—kicking millionaires when they—puffing up his chest when he is rejected by employers—pretty women—orphan children—

amidst the laughter of a hundred strangers—Camille beside you— laughing—snorting—then—in the silver light she seems to wipe her eyes—now you wrap your arm about her—you whisper—O my love— you—O my dear child—

Many nights now—your bed's emptiness—You listen to the house—ancient—rattling—You open your eyes—From her bedroom doorway you watch Camille sleep—when she does not stir—How close you creep—slight snores—then she—her feet—pale—small—How your heart pounds—Motionless you stand—breathless—waiting for her to wake—but she does not—

Your eyes—they—her body curled against yours—her head against your neck—warm breath—lips—her lank arms—her feet—your feet—She murmurs your name—you pull her against you—how her body—a tiny inferno—closer—closer—

Some nights I—my father—bearded and strong—his shirt sleeves rolled—laboring in the fields—fields of dirt—grasses—And sometimes he is with his goats—At the house, my mother waits for him—

What was her name?

I don't know—

Please try—

Sara—Ruth—

And what does she say to him—when he comes back?

She—

Does she ask about the goats—She—

She wonders about one goat in particular—Her belly—fat with life—

She whispers his name, what was it—

Jacob?

Maybe—

Yes, some nights—my father—my mother—how they were— younger than I am now—

Could they be alive somewhere—

And what if they live in a new house, and before them their family, their true family—

How old they are by now—

And perhaps in their dreams they remember me, as I was. This child—this—and then I was gone—And they wonder now if I am alive somewhere, and—

And maybe they imagine you—as you are now—and maybe someday your mother will see you on the street—and she won't even know why she starts crying—and your father—

And now I will sit in their kitchen—and here they will feed me—here they will hear of my days and I will hear of theirs—This man who is my brother—this woman who is my sister—this nephew—this niece—

All together again, finally—

When you awake—where Camille had been—now the coldness of absence—Nowhere in the great house—her breath—her—Nowhere in the fields—curled in the grasses—wounded—Flies—no—Now you call the name you gave her—how shrill your voice—panicked—Into the forest—what darkness—Here alone—what creatures—crooning and watching—

—vagrants on public benches—filthy—near starved—inebriated—The bottle of whisky you pass—lips—stink—You tell them about—They—their misfortunes—calamities—They expose their bellies and chests—pale scars—This was a bayonet—a heathen knife—This was my father, trying to murder me before I could grow old—devils in shadows—creatures moving beneath the soil—Perhaps that is where your little girl is—

—here a brown bear staggers—a woman's poodle dog—deranged with fear—sets upon its owner—gnashing—a fawn skitters into midday traffic—tangled steel—steam—glass cascading—

—skies blotted and no more stars—smog and steel—vapor trails—Where once—skeletons of steel—men like shadows—the human tide, men—choking inexhaustible—young girls in cheap smart dresses—faces garnished—riding on streetcars—clutching handbags—and in the evenings on their way to apartments—weary and yet free—They smile—laugh—The stained cigarettes they must smoke—The liquor they must drink—The gossip they must tell—The dreams they hold fast in their breasts—

—explosions in the city—numerous maimed—dying—dead—dust—smoke—stone—They say the aborigines in their wild militancy have done this—Natural anarchists—worse than animals—Later the police capture six militants—aborigines all—sheltered in the boarding schools—gun powder and pipes—A thousand people crowd the square to observe the hangings—One condemned man shouts the motto of the movement—He is jeered even as his neck is—

—O Joe—I—

You dismiss the cook—you tell her to take the driver—From a window you—When they take the automobile you—Good—

Here—flies—the spiders themselves—

I should burn this house down.

The windows and doors—boarded over—soon—The forest devours what—the trees break through the floors—vines—squirrels—wild dogs—

the driver's former shack—a blanket on the floor—there you lie—night advances over the land—the forest—eyes aglow—

You open your eyes—what was once the sun—Now a sliver of dead light—a black orb glowing—Her voice—no—The animals are howling in the darkness—

You close your eyes—a figure before you—slowly now the moonlight reveals—His arms outstretched—he moans—I have blood on my hands—in his cupped palm—a tiny flame—I know, Joe, you whisper—and then he is gone—

You close your eyes—a farm a thousand miles from any place you have ever called home—gray weathered building—cracked glass windows—nests in the ceilings—squirrels—mice—raccoons—skittering in the walls—acres of grassy fields—fences collapsing—Beyond the fences—a bounty of peopleless places—fields—forests—a mountain range over-looking—

now you return to a lean state—your skin cracked—hard—your hair sunbleached blonde—All your days in constant motion—hack-ing—hammering—a new fence—the building returned to—In the evenings—the sky reddens the horizon—Some hours you yearn for a drink—tobacco—but mostly you speak to yourself—the colors of the falling sun—the stars—the desperate noise of coyotes—owls—What mysteries—this place—

Now you—a tribe of goats—black and white—gray—brown—They call out in their horrific ways—milling—eating—You stroke them behind the ears—under the chins—they lick your face—cud stinking—One nuzzles your palm with a nose—hot—dripping—Another wags her tail—You do not name them yet you know them all the same—They follow you into the forest—sniffing and trotting—nibbling—flowers and grasses—The little ones springing about—And when you yearn to rest they lead you—a peak overlooking the valley—Now you doze against a rock while they—wise ancient faces—When you wake you call out—wordlessly—They follow at your heels—into the slow darkening—

The years—You grow melons—green and tangled in vines—dirt—
gnats—lines of heat—Your ledgers fill with notations such as—Melons this year fullest yet—an orchard perhaps—Sketches for systems
of irrigation—rotation of crops—Containers of manure—and ever
the goats—their generations—baying and milling—sniffing—trotting
ahead—

The wall—somewhere does—

—one night—your house seems to bend and distort—the walls—disappear—and in place—walls of stone—a man—upon a slate bench—leather skin—a loin cloth alone—Around him shadows—from torches unseen—You grasp your chest—your eyes—finally again as it before seemed—

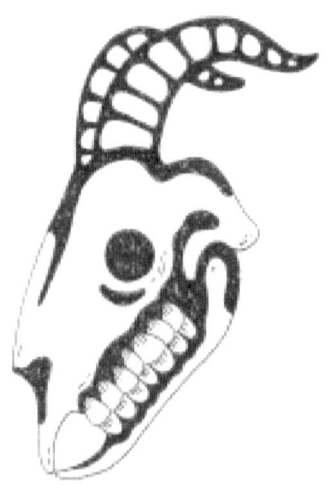

What line—smote—darkness—

On the final day you go into the mountains—you settle upon a ledge—
where you watch the day—And the goats nuzzle you—lick your face—
when you are slow to rise—You continue then along the path—

When—a cave—a gust of wind from within—and you enter—The goats
approach the opening and back away—their haunted cries—

Into the depths—From a corridor unseen a light—kindled—Here the
bones of bear and bison and dog—repose haphazard—frozen—shimmering with calcite—

Deeper—depictions of bison—lions—horses—creatures in gallop—
states of transition—Lions wearing hooves—Men bestowed with antlers—They appear to move and thrive in—shadows—

From the deeper corridors—drumbeats—voice rhythmic—the walls
flicker with motion—shadows—echoes—the voices of a dream—And
somewhere distant—a goat's cry—and then—

A voice—Come and see—

This has been an 𝕵𝖓𝖘𝖎𝖉𝖊 𝖙𝖍𝖊 𝕮𝖆𝖘𝖙𝖑𝖊 Crypt Edition reissue of Robert Kloss's novel The Woman Who Lived Amongst the Cannibals. Additionally, it is a text in the expanded field of literature and is catalogable as ITC-040 and under this heading as CRYPT-04. As with the original publication this volume is typeset in Abril, a modern slab serif typeface designed by José Scaglione and Veronika Burian. One could imagine it branded with fire into a piece of wood.

www.ingramcontent.com/pod-product-compliance
Lightning Source LLC
Chambersburg PA
CBHW031341070726
47496CB00017B/1411